RIDE TO THE GALLOWS

By the same author

The Secret of Lost Butte
Find Pecos Joe
Ride to Storm Town
Robbers in Rebel Grey
Rustlers' Moon
Timberland Vengeance
Scourge of the Rio Bravo
Blood at High Bend
The Herd Stealers

RIDE TO THE GALLOWS

JACK GREER

ROBERT HALE • LONDON

First published in Great Britain 1997

ISBN 0 7090 5981 7

Robert Hale Limited
Clerkenwell House
Clerkenwell Green
London EC1R 0HT

Typeset in Photina by Pitfold Design, Hindhead, Surrey.
Printed and bound in Great Britain by
WBC Book Manufacturers Ltd, Bridgend, Mid-Glamorgan.

ONE

Letting his horse amble along at its own pace, Pete Stannard entered Shelbyville, Colorado. Raising his eyes to the buildings about him, he slapped his right thigh and chuckled with pleasure. He hadn't seen Billy, his younger brother, in five years and tonight they would surely have themselves a night. They would indulge themselves in hours of chatter and laughter, and there would be cigars and whisky too. It did men good to relax over a bottle once in a while. Alcohol put a shine on success as nothing else could, and there was no doubt that Billy had become a real success here in Shelbyville. His general store was making money fast, he was a member of the town council, and he had a beautiful wife. Yes, sirree! Billy was doing fine, and he was hardly thirty yet. Give him another twenty years and where might he be? Washington? It wasn't impossible. Men of no less common birth had found their way into the Senate, and Billy had it in him!

Suddenly there was a loud crash nearby. Stannard jumped in his saddle, causing his mount to blow and veer. He spoke sharply to the horse, then glanced over to his right, asking himself what the tarnation that had been. Now he drew even with a gap in the buildings on the side to which he was peering, and he saw a brand new gallows standing there. The shocking noise had been made by the opening of the structure's trap and the dumping of a two hundred pound sack of grain at the rope's end. 'Yeah!' Stannard heard the man on the handle say. 'We done it all right. This'n will bust his neck out two feet long and leave him swingin' just like that there sack! Larn him, won't it?'

There were three other fellows up there with the guy beside the handle, and they haw-hawed hugely at the dreadful words their companion had just spoken. It was evident that they saw an execution as rare entertainment. Stannard took his eyes off the men. Let them gloat and caper. It was pretty awful really, and it made a man wonder what kind of society they had been brought up in. Breathing deeply, Stannard let go a sigh, and the elation of a minute ago left him with his breath. He supposed capital punishment was necessary, but he had never been a great believer in it, and he nudged his horse into a little trot that immediately took them past that rearing engine of doom, and he prayed inwardly that the condemned man, whoever he was, would find instant deliverance at the rope's end and be spared the pains of hell thereafter. Amen. And a pox on such as they who joyed in judicial murder!

Sitting firmly on his mount's spine, Stannard tried to shake off the sudden greyness of his mood and to some extent succeeded. The smile came back to his lips as he watched the buildings at the centre of Shelbyville growing larger on either hand. This place had the makings of a real town, though it would never amount to that much in the eyes of the present visitor – who, a natural traveller, had seen Chicago, New York, and the cities of the Old States – but it had a tendency to size and importance all the same, with its town hall, theatre, engineering establishment, stockyards and the rest. Then the rider spotted the legend, high up on a face of new bricks, which read: W. P. Stannard – Dry Goods and General. At the middle of the sign was a cornucopia, while at either end sat a pot of gold. Nicely! Young Bill had style all right; and you couldn't beat it.

Stannard turned in towards his brother's shop. He swung down at the rail outside it and threw a hitch. Then, leaving the animal, he swept off his hat and used it to beat the dust out of his garments, moving towards the door at the front of the store without pause. Then, just short of reaching the glass-panelled woodwork, he came to a stop and began to frown, for he saw a card in place behind the left-hand strip of glass which read: *Closed until further notice.*

Closed? This was a weekday, a working day – Thursday to be exact – and no shopkeeper in the whole country worthy of his salt would close up indefinitely while there was profit to be had. Stannard scratched his head; he just didn't get it. There was this image of brother Billy, presenting himself as the original slave to his work, while here was a closed store in a town that looked as if it had plenty of dollars to spend. Something must be seriously wrong. Illness, perhaps. Or maybe there'd been a death among the in-laws. No doubt the explanation would prove simple enough, but it was a bit disconcerting to be confronted by that uncompromising notice nevertheless. You had to use words carefully. They were damned funny things.

So what ought he to do now? Stannard figured he'd go round to the back yard. He could see an alley running down the shop's right-hand side, and it plainly served a rear entrance to the premises. If there was anybody at home, a knock would arouse them; and, if the property was indeed deserted for now, he would just have to find himself somewhere in town to wait until the master and his missus did come home. That's all there was to that.

Stannard moved to the head of the alley and strolled towards the yard at the back of the property, stepping into it and turning left just as a shapely and rather beautiful young woman – if you liked them very dark and grave-looking, and Stannard did – came out of the back door, a key in her hand, and turned her head to look at him with eyes that held a faint surprise. 'Who are you?' she asked crisply.

'Merle?' he hazarded, supposing this girl his brother's wife; for, though he had been told often enough in letters that his sister-in-law was the loveliest of women, he had never seen her likeness.

A small frown gathered upon the girl's brow and she shook her head. 'No, I'm Iris Bates.'

Stannard sent his mind ferreting back among the half-forgotten scraps of information concerning Bill's in-laws that he had mentally filed away when his brother's letters had first begun to recount Bill's courtship of Merle Bates. 'Ah, the – the half-sister,' he said uncertainly, fearing at once that he had committed a gaffe of sorts.

'Sister,' the dark girl corrected that mite too firmly. 'Are you Peter Stannard, Bill's brother, by any chance? You answer the description he gave.'

'Yes, I'm Pete.'

Iris Bates nodded. 'Merle and I never allowed that half-sister business. It was mother's affair.'

'I'm sure I want to know nothing of it,' Stannard said, recalling that element of family shame and dismissing it as just one of those things. 'Where's Bill?'

The girl gave a start, her breasts standing high within the white lace front of her purple silk dress as she appeared unable to breathe out. 'You don't know, do you?'

'Know what?' Stannard queried, vaguely recalling the past tense which the dark girl had used when speaking of Merle and herself a few moments ago. 'What's up? There's something wrong, isn't there?'

'You weren't summoned here?'

'Who by?'

'Your brother – or his lawyers?'

'Bill's lawyers?' Stannard echoed, more puzzled than ever.

'The men from Canon City who defended him.'

'Defended him!' Stannard yelled. 'What the hell is this? I'm a riding man, and I haven't had a permanent address in years. Bill and I used to correspond through post offices. I haven't picked up a letter from him in six months. This visit to Shelbyville was intended to be a surprise.'

'Then it seems that you're the one who's likely to be surprised,' Iris Bates observed rather grimly. 'Oh, this is —'

'What?'

'This is awful!' the girl responded. 'I can't believe chance alone brought you here. I believe I can see the devil's hand at work in all this.'

There was something terrible coming. Stannard could feel it in every fibre of his being. But they could not keep on fencing like this – with the reluctance of the one striking sparks off the mounting fear of the other. 'Tell me,' he commanded sharply.

'I'm going to,' she said, pushing open the back door of the house again. 'Let's go indoors. You need in sit down, and so do I. This isn't going to be easy for either of us.'

'Iris – I may call you that?'

'Of course.'

'Is Merle dead?'

'Yes.'

'Bill?'

'Billy is alive – for now.'

'For now?' Stannard heard the trapdoor of the gallows crash open again and saw that sack of grain swinging. 'For now? What do you mean by that? Speak, dammit!'

She stepped indoors, more or less compelling him to follow her, and he walked into a cold kitchen, with a blackleaded fireplace to his right, armchairs on either side of the hearth, table, sideboard, and rugs about the floor, the whole somehow conveying an impression of departed felicity and adding a deathlike quality to the faces that stared out of the faded pictures around the walls.

Iris Bates pointed to the chair on the right of the hearth and said: 'Now, Peter – please don't get angry with me. Nothing that has happened is my fault. Can we speak together calmly?'

Stannard went to the chair indicated and seated himself. 'As I rode into Shelbyville,' he said, 'I saw some workmen testing a gallows that they had just finished building.'

'For Bill,' she said. 'He is to hang there at noon on Saturday.'

'This Saturday?'

'Yes.'

'Bill killed Merle?'

'Yes.'

'Great God!' Stannard breathed. 'This isn't happening. I'm asleep. This is a nightmare. I'm dreaming it all!'

'If only you were,' Iris Bates said heavily. 'Your brother has been tried and sentenced. He murdered his wife. It was an open and shut case.'

'No-no-no!' Stannard protested desperately. 'I can't believe a word of it. Bill would never have killed his wife. Bill would never kill anybody. There never was never a kinder or gentler man. I'm the one in our family with the raw streak!'

'Even so – '

'Bill actually confessed to murder?'

'He didn't deny it,' Iris said dismally. 'Do please remember that we're talking about my sister. They were on the landing, having a row, and Bill admitted that he pushed her. Merle went tumbling down the stairs. I found her lying in the hall. The back of her head was crushed in.'

'You found her,' Stannard said aghast. 'This gets worse and worse. Tell me all about it.'

Iris Bates nodded. She sat there for a few moments

gathering her thoughts. Then she explained how it had been her habit to visit her brother-in-law's house most afternoons, just after lunch, and sit with her sister Merle for an hour or two, discussing their own or family affairs – or just plain gossiping – while Bill Stannard had been at work in the store and the women had had time for leisure. On the afternoon of Merle's death, however, Iris had approached the front of the shop from the street – intending to pass through it as usual and enter the living quarters from the direction of the store itself, when she had found the front door locked and been able to detect no sign of activity beyond. So, exercising a blood relation's normal freedom of access, she had walked round to the back – much as Pete Stannard had himself done just now – and entered Merle's home through the rear door, passing on, when she found the kitchen deserted, into the hall itself, where she had come upon her sister lying with her head driven up against the leg of a heavy wooden table which supported a big glazed pot which held an aspidistra. Merle was dead and, judging from the semi-congealed state of the great pool of blood spread around her, had been for the better part of an hour.

The dark woman made no bones about the shock that the sight had caused her, and admitted that it had taken several minutes to wear off; but she had eventually recovered enough to go and fetch Doctor Hugh Banff – who had supposed at first, like Iris herself, that an accident had occurred – but then the medico had spotted a bruise on the point of Merle's jaw and become suspicious that the dead woman had been punched down the stairs rather than fallen as had appeared the case to begin with. This had led to the sheriff being summoned and an inquiry instituted, and almost at once Bill Stannard – who had been located in the Gunpowder saloon – had admitted to pushing his wife so that she had fallen down the stairs, though he had added that she had been sitting up and no more than a little dazed when he had stormed out of the building, locking the front door in his wake.

'But – but don't you see?' Pete Stannard spluttered at the girl seated opposite him. 'That's – that's what I told you. Bill would never kill anybody. What happened sounds to me like a marital spat that ended in an – an accident.'

'Stop deceiving yourself,' Iris advised. 'The jury didn't see it like that. An assault had occurred, and they were satisfied that Merle had died of it. That's murder.'

The fact was too clear to be argued over, and Stannard could only throw up his hands in defeat and plead: 'But even allowing it did happen like that, Iris, you couldn't call it premeditated murder. Not murder in the first degree.'

'Again,' Iris said patiently, 'you don't know all. Bill had said several times in public that he was going to kill his wife for her goings on.'

'Damn fool!' Stannard almost sobbed. 'They found him in a god-damned saloon too!'

'He'd been drinking a lot around that time,' said the girl with the black hair and ivory-tinted features. 'Alice Mears, the woman who owns the Gunpowder saloon, is a great one at drawing out troubled men. She's no good, but she's got what it takes with the other half. Bill had told her everything. The evidence she gave about his state of mind was conclusive.'

'Bill never drank when I had a place in his life.'

'He'd learned.'

'I've yet to get all this straight,' Stannard admitted. 'Merle had been consorting with other men? Was that the cause of the trouble between her and Bill?'

Iris Bates stared over her caged fingers at the floor. Stannard realised that she could not find words with which to answer him. She didn't wish to condemn her sister, while she was still trying to go easy on him. 'Spit it out, Iris!' he snapped. 'Don't try to spare anybody. Let's just have the facts. I am getting riled now!'

'All right,' Iris Bates said. 'Merle had been seeing other men.'

'Oh, heck!'

'It's hard to excuse.'

'There is no excuse,' Stannard said hotly. 'You vow to stick to the one.'

'We should try to understand.'

'Understand what?'

'Merle had a strong liking for men,' Iris explained. 'She was never a little Goody Two-Shoes. She'd had lots of beaux. Even at school she went with boys and did things she shouldn't. I thought Bill knew about all that, but it seems he didn't. He told me later he married Merle believing her as pure as the driven snow. I warned him that he would have to be a man and accept his wife for how she was. But Merle's virtue was Bill's Achilles heel, and he couldn't close his mind to her unfaithfulness.'

'He worshipped her!' Stannard declared. 'I know that from what his letters said.'

'Perhaps that was the trouble,' Iris sighed. 'Men worship goddesses. Merle was very much a woman. She let everybody down, herself included. But that was Merle, Peter.'

'And now she's gone.'

'It will be the same with your brother by this time on Saturday.'

Yes, Bill would be dead and buried Stannard inwardly reflected, shuddering. 'Less than two days left to him. I must try to do something. I can't let him die like a dog! If Bill said he left Merle alive and no more than dazed, then that's how it was.'

'The bruise on her jaw?'

'Bill might have pushed her,' Stannard contended, 'but I'd stake my own life he'd never have socked her. Why, George Washington was mighty close to being a liar compared with Bill. I know I'm repeating myself, Iris, but if my brother said something happened a certain way, you can rely on it that it did. They had a row – married folk do. He pushed her out of his path – husbands have been known to do that. She fell down the stairs and knocked herself scatty. That's not unheard of either. She lay dazed, but unhurt in any real sense, and he walked out of the house and left her. Pretty standard also. Hey?'

Iris showed him her palms, her shoulders twitching slightly.

'Isn't that the story as you gave it me?' Stannard asked. 'I've only added what's reasonable.'

'Billy has been tried,' Iris Bates said, 'found guilty, and been sentenced to hang. Far cleverer people than you and me were involved in his arrest and trial. You've come straight into this business, without having heard a thing – or not having given the matter any real thought – and you seem to want to tell me that you know more about what happened in this house than the folk who were actually involved in the investigation. Do please try to reverse the situation, and then ask yourself how you would answer me.'

'I've faith in my brother,' Stannard said resolutely, 'and that's what makes me speak as I do. Bill didn't murder his wife. I think somebody else did. What happened between Merle and him was used as a frame.'

Iris Bates looked at him as if she could not believe

that she was hearing aright. 'You must be out of your mind!' she informed him. 'Somebody else did it! Who? Madness! You are asking for trouble, Peter Stannard, and Shelbyville will give it to you. Be sensible now. Go and say goodbye to Bill. Then ride on. You could be in Durango by Saturday.'

'No,' Stannard said, now at his quietest and most controlled. 'My heart tells me that Bill didn't murder his wife. Somebody else came in here, perhaps found Merle still down, and finished the job. I aim to prove it happened like that, and bring the true culprit in before twelve noon on Saturday. This I will do, Iris Bates. Mark me well!'

The girl opened her mouth to protest again, but he waved her silent.

TWO

The silence hung between the pair for a long moment, throbbing with the drama of Stannard's pose; and then Iris Bates rose from her chair and said: 'I think we should leave. I have permission to come in here and keep the dust down, but not to use the house as a convenience.'

Stannard rose also, easing his saddle-stiffened knees and grimacing. 'Hold on,' he said, putting a plea into his voice. 'I may not get the chance to come into this house again. Show me where Merle died. That won't upset your conscience or anybody else's sense of fitness, will it?'

The dark girl gave her head a slight shake, then faced about. 'It happened through there – in the hall.'

'Show me.'

Iris walked to the door set in the wall at the back of the room. Opening it, she left the way clear for Stannard to join her – which he did without hesitation – and he found himself in a broad but gloomy passage which appeared to cross the entire dwelling and have exits at either end. A number of doorways – obviously the entrances to various rooms – were visible within the walls on either hand, and the stairs themselves were central to the area. The steps were few and rose to a landing on the floor above, while it was also clear that other stairways existed and served the higher levels of this tall property unseen from here. 'Well, that's no great tumble,' Stannard observed, glancing up the ten steps that issued into the hall itself. 'So what was it they said Merle struck her head against and sustained that mortal injury?'

'This,' Iris said, putting out a hand and touching the very solidly constructed mahogany table which stood backed up against the wall opposite the foot of the stairs. 'I did tell you about it.'

Stannard walked over to the table and passed a brooding eye all over it, though his interest centred as much upon the blue glazed pot which occupied its top as anything else. He looked closely at the packed earth which the pot contained and the aspidistra that grew out of the soil. 'I can see no sign that the dirt in the pot was cracked or loosened by the force of the impact which would have been created by Merle's head driving into the table. Nor do I see any traces of embedded blood around either. You must have done a rare good job of cleaning up in here.'

'The best that I possibly could,' the girl answered.

'The table's mahogany,' Stannard remarked.

'That's among the hardest woods you'll find. It will always put a dent in paint and plaster!'

'I'm well aware of all that,' Iris Bates said. 'The table was stood fast against the wall to begin with. The plaster wasn't actually hit by the edge of the tabletop but simply absorbed the impact.'

Stannard muttered doubtfully. 'It takes a real heavy blow to break the average human skull. With such a one as you tell me slew Merle, there ought to be clear signs of a collision around.'

'It happened,' Iris said shortly. 'It's silly to insist on details. Do they matter that much?'

'Yes, they do,' Stannard responded with the same shortness. 'You know what I'm getting at. If Merle's head didn't strike the table hard enough to bust it open, she was clearly hit by something else that did.'

'It did strike the table hard enough, Peter. You're trying to make this come out how you want it to.'

'All I hear from you, Iris, is what you've been told. Is that the same as what you think?'

'Do I have to keep reminding you,' the dark girl demanded, 'that it was I who found Merle lying dead in here?'

'So what?'

'She had been punched. You really must keep a grip on the facts. Or is it that you're just a stupidly obstinate man?'

'You're getting rude.'

'You speak your mind, and I'm speaking mine.'

'Pshaw!'

'I'm trying to save you from yourself!' the girl warned him. 'You're being foolhardy. Everything we've talked about was brought up during the trial. You want to see the evidence one way, but the jury was otherwise convinced. I liked Bill. I always found him one of the best and kindest of men. He helped many, and deserves to be helped. But it's got past that now. There's no doubt he killed Merle. If you had got here a week ago, you could have added your weight to the plea for clemency that was sent to the governor. As it stands, that appeal was turned down. It's too late to attempt anything further in that line. Tod Hempnall, the hangman from Canon City, is due in town tomorrow to test the rope. At noon on Saturday he will do his duty.'

'With a blessing from you?'

'She was my sister,' Iris Bates said unhappily.

'Half-sister,' Stannard insisted, grimly hurtful, 'and not much of a woman at that.'

'You shall not judge her!' Iris Bates cried angrily. 'I've put up with you until now – because Bill is your brother and I know how you must feel – but now I've had enough of you and him. He's a guilty man, Peter, and he deserves to hang. Fornication is an ugly thing, but murder is a far worse one!'

'You want my brother to swing!' Stannard stormed at her. 'You want revenge!'

'That's cruel and bitterly untrue!' the dark girl

denied, raging in her turn. 'I won't listen to any more of it. I've told you what's best for you. Leave town – go!'

'Not on your life!' Stannard retorted. 'I'm more than ever determined to stay. Bill has been abandoned. It isn't just a matter of judge and jury. You, as seems to be the case with everybody else, believe him guilty in your heart. You don't want mercy for him – you want punishment. I can see it clearly. Shelbyville wants Bill Stannard's life!'

'He made his own bed,' the girl fired back, 'and now he must lie upon it. I regret what he did – and you regret what must happen to him – but Bill has only himself to blame. He brought his own fate down upon his head – wilfully – and he must suffer alone.'

'Die alone?'

'Yes,' Iris Bates said. 'You goaded me, and now you've heard all my mind. That's it. Will you go, please?'

Stannard felt the temptation to keep it up. The girl was unfeeling in his opinion and he wanted to make her feel as bad as he felt himself. For that moment he hated the law and the whole human race. Iris Bates was a picture of anger, defiance – and even fear. He realised that he was very close to alienating her for good, and he doubted that ever again there could be even a hint of friendship between them. Yet she was his only link with this town and the crime itself, and if he did indeed stick around – in the role of master detective – he might very well need her mind and contacts to give him any chance at all of solving the mystery of his sister-in-law's death. So, smiling at her in the degree that he could manage, he gestured his resignation and said: 'You're right, I guess. It's hard sure enough, but when hard's all there is, hard it has to be.'

'Now you're seeing sense,' the dark girl acknowledged, sounding greatly relieved and shepherding him back into the kitchen, where she stayed him with a tug at his shirt. 'Peter, if you want to see Bill for one last time, I'll go to the jailhouse with you and explain to Sheriff Joe Temple who you are. It could make a difference. Joe and I have walked out together. He's a tough nut, and liable to send you packing, but I have more influence with him than most.'

'That's right nice of you, Iris,' Stannard said. 'When were you thinking of – for the visit?'

'Why, now.'

'I reckon tomorrow evening will be time for it,' Stannard said carefully.

Iris Bates's face hardened again. 'You're still hell bent, Peter.'

'Please, Iris!' he begged. 'I can't just ride away. I'd have to live with myself afterwards. Don't you see that?'

'I know what you're up to,' she accused. 'You're taking the heat out of this. You want to use me. You say one thing but you mean another.'

'Maybe,' he admitted. 'But I'm not trying to include you in anything. Whatever I do will be done on my own responsibility.'

Iris flapped a contemptuous hand in front of his face. 'What is it you want to know?'

'Who was the last man Merle was involved with?'

'Luke Barnes, our mayor.'

'Anybody else she'd been doing Bill dirt with since her marriage?'

'Phil Lemming along at the stagecoach office,' she replied, 'but I don't think that went on for long. There was Clifford Sandford too. He's the manager over at Virgil Hardiman's Toppling M ranch, and his employer's pet.' She gave a stamp with her right foot. 'I know the truth of these things, but it harrows me to tell it. Even the dead have the right to their privacy.'

'Lemming and Sandford, eh? Either of those two have any sort of motive for killing Merle?'

'No.'

'What about their wives?'

'Cliff Sandford has no wife, and Lemming has a sick one.'

'Is there a Mrs Barnes?'

'Liz Barnes wouldn't hurt a fly,' Iris Bates answered. 'Murder is a male crime. Men don't bring life into the world. They have no idea how valuable it is.'

Stannard nodded slowly over what had just been said. Yet he wasn't altogether sure that murder was a male preserve. He'd heard tell of females who were dab-hands with axe and poison bottle. Anyhow, his interest had abruptly settled elsewhere. On the mantelpiece to be exact. For there was something there that didn't quite add up. Perhaps it was of absolutely no importance whatsoever, but right then his mind was alive with suspicions and he was sensitive to possibilities which normally would not have registered on his intelligence at all. Just one of those tall brass candlesticks? Possible, he supposed. But didn't they always come in twos?

He studied the mantelpiece some more. There were china ornaments all along its length, with the single candlestick of solid brass standing at the centre. The holder was an impressive item. It was undoubtedly European, and probably German; but it was not so much the size or design of the brass piece that troubled Stannard's mind as the fact that he had seen their like in a number of households and they were usually placed as stops at either end of the kind of ornamentation which the mantelpiece before him possessed. For all her lightness of the leg, Stannard could well imagine that his late sister-in-law had been a fastidious woman domestically who would have sought to have everything exactly right in her home. If two candlesticks were the fashion, then two candlesticks it would have had to have been. One at either end of the shelf – and the thought of one in the middle would have been an unendurable pain. So, assuming there had been two candlesticks to begin with, where was the second one now? 'That brass candlestick,' he suddenly felt constrained to say. 'Did it originally come as one of a pair?'

'How on earth would I know?' the girl demanded, plainly disconcerted. 'Why do you bother with a question like that?'

'I've seen them set up on mantelpieces as endstops.'

'Is that all?'

'Not by a long chalk,' Stannard confided. 'A candlestick of the size and weight of that yonder would serve as a perfect club. Just right to smash a skull in.'

'That's a horrible thought!' Iris Bates declared.

'You can say that again!' Stannard acknowledged. 'I expect you can see why I'm asking if that candlestick on the shelf was one of a pair?'

'You're saying,' Iris said, 'if there was another it could have been used to kill Merle. No, I'm fairly sure there was never a second candlestick on the mantelpiece.'

'Only fairly sure?' Stannard queried. 'That isn't a certainty, Iris. The dusting in here has been your job.'

'Not for that long, nor many times. Now I come to think of it, I'm sure there's never been more than the one brass candlestick in this room.'

'So now you are sure. How long has that piece been up there?'

'Not long,' Iris said, blinking as if images were now

rising into her mind unbidden. 'Only since around the time of Merle's death. Yes, I'm sure that's correct. I'd never considered it before. Had no reason to, I guess, and can't believe there's any significance to it now.'

'Yet there could have been two?' Stannard asked, picking his words with care and trying to get over his exact meaning. 'Perhaps first stood up there around the time of Merle's death? Even on the actual day? Sounds improbable, I know, but these things do happen.'

'It is possible,' the dark girl admitted. 'More than that I wouldn't like to say.'

Iris Bates plucked at Stannard's shirt again. This time she passed him and drew him onwards. Then she stepped out of the back door and into the yard, Stannard moving in her wake and treading beyond her as she turned to use the key that she had been holding to the lock when her companion had first come upon her. Watching while she locked up, he said: 'Where do you live, Iris – in case I need to call round?'

'I live at Yellow Gables, Fore Street,' the girl answered. 'You turn left on leaving this house and walk a short way down the street. My home is plain to see. The colour speaks for itself.'

'Got you,' he said, as they headed into the passage at the side of the house and then towards the street.

'I expect you'll knock on my door when you want to see Bill.'

'I wonder if I'll need to trouble you,' Stannard said. 'The sheriff will probably accept who I am without any fuss.'

'Please yourself,' the girl returned. 'It could make it easier for you, that's all. Please remember that you are a stranger in a strange town, and be careful when you start asking questions. You're abrasive, and you do have a tendency to offend.'

'Thanks,' Stannard said, grinning crookedly as they halted beside the rail to which his horse was tied. 'I'll be careful what I say, and try to be sure that I can trust anybody I speak to.'

'You know nobody,' Iris insisted. 'Where can you go?'

'The Gunpowder saloon?' he suggested. 'I might get something out of Alice Mears.'

'Much good you'll do yourself there!'the dark girl sniffed. 'Alice was Merle's best friend. She wants to see Bill executed as much as anybody in this town. I think Alice would be best left alone.'

Stannard made no comment. He was well aware of what he was undertaking and that he was likely to meet with more kicks than kind words. But it was all a matter of resolution, and he had resolved to pull off a miracle. Somehow he was going to save his brother from the gallows, and he had as much faith in himself as he had in Bill's innocence. He feared the bad offices of neither man nor woman, and believed with all his heart that heaven would not let an innocent man hang. If Iris Bates disliked him a little less, she might comprehend that, for all his bluntness and forceful manner, he was a genuine fellow. In the end truth always begot the truth. Alice Mears and her like notwithstanding. 'Obliged to you for your help, Iris,' he said, 'and I'll remember where you live.'

'Do that, Peter,' the dark girl responded, turning away from him and walking off down the street.

Stannard gazed stoically after her retreating shape. It would have been so much nicer if she had wished him 'good luck'.

THREE

Stannard recalled having glimpsed the Gunpowder saloon while riding into town earlier on. The drinking house was situated a hundred yards back to his right and not far from the spot where he had seen the newly erected gallows being tested. Now, freeing his horse from the rail and catching it at the mouth, he walked the animal back over the rutted main street to the place where the saloon stood, tethering it again when he reached the hitching rail which ran across the front of the establishment. Then, standing on the sidewalk for a few moments, he rolled himself a cigarette and composed a little speech for Alice Mears, whipping a match across the seat of his canvas pants and lighting up as he shouldered open the batwings and went indoors.

It was at once evident to Stannard that the Gunpowder saloon was much better than the average of its kind. The floor was clean, the paint was reasonably new, the tables and chairs were numerous and well-placed, and the gambling equipment – which included a big chuck-a-luck wheel – was all in sound condition. Even the barkeeper was a superior type, being slim, youngish, carefully shaven, pomaded with fragrant oil, and good-looking in a craggy sort of way. He also had a ready smile, which shone forth like his newly starched white apron, and his voice was polite and well-modulated as he asked: 'What will you have, sir?'

'A light beer,' Stannard replied. 'Is Alice Mears in the place?'

'She is, sir. I reckon she's through in her living room.'

'Could you let her know there's a guy out here who'd like to speak with her?'

'Why, surely,' the barkeeper said. 'Miss Mears will want to know your name and business.'

'My name is Peter Stannard. I'm the brother of the Bill Stannard this town is fixing to hang. My business concerns that same Bill Stannard.'

'That's plain enough,' said the man behind the bar; and he raised a hand to a leering, spidery figure, with a round, wicked eye and a twisted mouth to match, who was sitting beside a doorway at the back of the room and now identified as a guard of sorts. 'Will you see to it, Manea?'

The man with the leering features rose into a shape that was seemingly still half coiled and, opening the door on his left, vanished into a passage which the swinging woodwork had partially revealed.

'You there!' called a voice from Stannard's back.

Stannard slowly faced about, his gaze fixing on a big, darkly handsome young man, perfectly groomed and tailored – but with the flush and puffy marks of dissipation upon his cheeks – who was seated on a tilted chair at the room's central table and had a glass of bourbon at his lips. 'Me?'

The big man nodded curtly, then sipped his liquor and put his glass down. 'Did I hear your name aright?'

'Stannard – Pete Stannard.'

'Hear that?' queried the big fellow, sharing a raised eyebrow between the two hardbitten characters dressed in range garments who were occupying the table with him. 'He's the brother of that misbegotten piece of scum who's sitting in our jail and waiting for Tod Hempnall to drop him into hell!'

'Mister,' Stannard said evenly, 'you have a gift for words, but you should use it more carefully.'

'Prefer privy to scum?' the other taunted. 'Well, you've the same looks as our Stannard. Do you murder women too?'

Stannard tut-tutted, holding on to his temper. 'This early in the day too.'

'What do you mean?'

'You're drunk.'

'That's an insult.'

'No, it's a fact.'

'I've a good mind to get up and shoot you!'

'You know what they say about a good mind,' Stannard reminded. 'Don't change it.'

'Why, you – !' the other began, lurching to his feet and sweeping back the skirts of his jacket as he went for his gun.

Stannard knew exactly how to deal with this. His pistol seemed to leap into his hand. The other had barely touched his Colt as yet and, freezing, simply stood there now. Cocking his weapon, Stannard grinned coldly. 'Too easy,' he said, the sneer in his voice not appearing on his face. 'Now that's a fancy gun you're wearing. Silver-chased barrel and ivory grip. Custom-made, eh? You're a lucky man to have that kind of money to spend.' His features hardened. 'Using your first finger and thumb on the butt, I want you to draw that fine weapon carefully and drop it in the spittoon beside your table – because that's where it belongs. Do it – now!'

The big man jumped at the sudden snap in Stannard's voice. 'I'll – I'll see you at the devil first!' he spluttered.

'That's your destination,' Stannard acknowledged, closing in upon the central table and its occupants, his revolver steady in his grasp. 'But I won't be joining you there for a while.'

'Do your worst!' came back the challenge.

Stannard didn't mind being defied by a man who was up to it, but this one clearly wasn't. The big guy was simply waiting for his companions to come to his defence. 'Careful, gents,' he advised. 'He isn't worth it.'

'Get him then, you damned cowards!'

Past caring by now, Stannard thrust the muzzle of his gun against his enemy's forehead and said: 'Either that fancy Colt goes into the spittoon – or I scatter your brains all over the room. What's it to be? You've a second only!'

The ivory-handled Colt clattered into the spittoon, and its owner sat down hard, flushed and badly scared. 'I'll have your jobs for this!' he croaked at his companions. 'What kind of men are you?'

'Sensible ones,' Stannard advised. 'The cemetery is damned inhospitable, and it only takes long-staying guests.'

'You long son-of-a- bitch!'

'For heaven's sake, Cliff!' protested the older of the two hardbitten men sitting with the big one. 'You are drunk. That guy's going to kill you if you keep it up. It ain't worth it, sir! I know how you felt about Merle Stannard, but – but it ain't worth it. She's dead and gone, and they're going to hang her killer. Don't you want to be alive for the show on Saturday?'

'Tell him,' Stannard agreed. 'He was never closer to getting measured for his box than he was a minute ago!'

'No, don't tell him, Bart!' urged a woman's voice from Stannard's right. 'Enough's been said already.

That goes for you especially, Cliff Sandford. You may be the boss on Virgil Hardiman's Toppling A, but I say what goes in here. As for you, Stannard, put up your gun and simmer down!'

'I have the right to be angry!' Stannard declared, scowling at the tall blonde who was bracing him. 'So that's Clifford Sandford, eh? I've heard his name. He's clearly all mouth and not much else, and he needs to learn a lesson or two in how to behave himself.'

'So do you!' the blonde retorted contemptuously. 'You were roaring off like some old bear with a belly full of strychnine. I told you to put that gun away. If you don't do it, you won't get to talk with me.'

'Very well,' Stannard said, and spun his six-shooter into leather. 'There. Does that suit?'

The blonde nodded, apparently satisfied. 'Cliff, get out – and take Bart Hengel and John Smith with you!'

'There's no need for that, Alice!' Sandford protested.

The tall woman moved deeper into the bar-room, the backs of her hands shooing. 'Go, boys!' she urged. 'We'll be pleased to see you again – tomorrow.'

Sandford shrugged, said something about getting a drink elsewhere, and got up, gesturing for the two men with him to do the same, and the trio left the middle table and made for the way out. The woman watched them go, as did Stannard too; then, with the batwings still flapping behind them, she turned away, beckoning, and Stannard pursued her through the doorway once more guarded by the evil-looking

Manea and into the back of the building, where they crossed a corridor and entered a room that had been tastefully furnished as a parlour.

Now the blonde halted in front of a fireplace hidden by a Chinese screen and, facing into the room, considered the slightly hangdog Stannard, a faint smile coming to her hard but very beautiful face. 'You can call me Alice or Miss Mears,' she said. 'Take your pick, sir.'

'Thank you, Miss Mears.'

'Not at all, Mr Stannard.'

He smiled wryly at his toes. 'Settled that, haven't we?'

'You wanted a word with me?'

'Yes.'

'Do sit down.'

'I'll stay on my feet if you don't mind,' Stannard said, beginning to prowl a little. 'When you ride a horse, the horse gets all the right exercise.'

Alice Mears sank down into a chair made of bent cane and plaited raffia, her left hand reaching out and its fingers running momentarily over the lower notes of the richly encased square piano standing close by. 'We don't have to be enemies, Mr Stannard. Your brother and I liked each other well enough.'

'Yet you want him hanged.'

'I haven't said so.'

Frowning, Stannard looked into the flowered glass of the mirror which hung above the fireplace and the fierce violet eyes in his lean, swarthy face returned the harshness of his mood. 'Somebody else said it for you.'

'Iris?' Alice Mears asked acutely. 'It would have had to have been Iris Bates.'

Stannard nodded reluctantly. He saw little point in denying a confidence which he had already betrayed.

'You've met her,' the blonde stated. 'Did she send you to me?'

'No. She mentioned your name and saloon in passing, that's all. I gathered that Bill used to come into your saloon and drown his sorrows.'

'Seems a lot gets said in passing,' Alice Mears observed ironically. 'You might say Bill cried on my shoulder a little, yes. He didn't have to come in here. He was a friend, but Merle was my best friend.'

'I'd gathered that too,' Stannard admitted. 'What went wrong between him and Merle? I'd like to hear your opinion of it. I suspect you'd have a better understanding of it than anybody.'

'Too much business and too little bed.'

Stannard blinked. He would have preferred to believe that he had misunderstood her, but realised that he had not. 'That's kind of blunt and to the point.'

Alice smoothed down the skirt of her orange dress, and her petticoats whispered silkily beneath it, while her eardrops swung and the semi-precious stones of her necklace glittered dully against the skin under her throat. 'I say it as I see it, Mr Stannard; that's how I am. I make no distinction between men and women. Girls talk about their love lives as much as men do. If a man and his wife aren't happy in bed, they won't be happy anywhere.'

'Is that so?' Stannard mused. 'Sounds to me like Merle was just another wanton.'

'I hoped you were bright enough to grasp that I was saying just the opposite,' Alice said, a disappointed sigh coming through in her voice. 'Merle was the nearest thing to a sister I've ever had. She wasn't perfect, but neither are you and I. She'd have made Bill a good wife if he'd been a better husband. She tried.'

'But not hard enough maybe.'

'What's wrong with a woman wanting a social life?' Alice Mears asked indignantly. 'What's wrong with her enjoying the company of men? Merle had a head on her shoulders; she was not some downtrodden little mouse. I found her a person after my own heart. She and I could have always carved out a place for ourselves in the world of men. I miss her. Yes, by heaven, I do!' Her brow gathered and her lips compressed, while her shoulders heaved a little. Then it burst from her. 'That brute of a Bill!'

'You do want him hung,' Stannard said bitterly. 'Of course you do!'

'There was no need to kill her!' the blonde snapped in reply. 'He must have been aware that there had been other men before him. It was up to him to keep her straight – to do right by her. Love is just an illusion; and the physical side of it is just like all the other physical things about us. They have to be looked to in order that we may live. It's no good getting possessive.' She tossed her head arrogantly. 'That was Billy's worst fault – he was too possessive. I hope you're not like that?'

'I'm damned if I know,' Stannard confessed. 'I've never been forced to find out. Women have played a small part in my life. I've travelled some and worked plenty. That's been about it.' He narrowed an eye reflectively. 'I wouldn't like a girl I loved to be unfaithful to me; but I don't think I'd kill her for it. Fact is, Miss Mears, I'm sure Bill didn't either.'

Alice Mears gave a visible start and stared at him hard, an understanding that was also highly resistant to his mind appearing in her eyes. 'I figured that might be it,' she said. 'You want to prove your brother innocent. Innocent he is not. It's too late anyhow. Bill was virtually convicted out of his own mouth. He must have told me twenty times that he'd kill Merle if she didn't alter her ways.'

'I can just hear him saying it,' Stannard admitted sourly. 'Bill has a rash streak in him, and he's liable to spit out things like that. But he doesn't mean them. It's all talk – anger – frustration. I said as much to Iris Bates.'

'Anger and frustration don't lead to murder?' the blonde inquired sapiently. 'Oh, I think they do. Iris

Bates can't help you, and neither can I. Nobody can. Not how you're almost begging to be helped right now.'

Stannard clenched his fists, and turned his head aside, blowing hard. That had been wickedly unfair. He was seeking enlightenment, yes – and practical help if he could get it – but begging for the pity of others he was not. That would demean not only him but Bill too; and he was determined that, whatever the outcome of this terrible business, he would leave his own and his brother's pride intact. If he did that, a relationship might end but the memory of it would remain unsullied. A man only truly died when he was forgotten. Or so Stannard wished to believe just then.

With his humiliation still eating at him, Stannard walked slowly to a window at the back of the room and gazed out. He saw waste ground beyond the glass. There was an ugly emptiness about its clayey expanse. It was surrounded by properties, among which he he could make out his brother Bill's, and there was an unfinished well upon it that seemed to attract him strangely in that moment and scar his soul with its presence.

'If I've been told aright,' Stannard now blurted suddenly, since he feared that he might otherwise say something critical of the home setting of the woman who sat watching him, 'Merle's last love affair was with your mayor, a man called Warnes. Would that be correct?'

'I believe so. What about it?'

'Did Merle turn to Warnes straight after favouring Sandford?'

'Again, as far as I know,' Alice Mears said.

'How did Sandford like that?'

'He didn't like it. You must be well aware of that. It seemed to me he'd given you good reason.'

Stannard nodded. He supposed that he had been on the receiving end of some of the ranch manager's previously unexpressed ire. 'Maybe he was playing the hurt lover just now, but was he anywhere around at the time Merle was murdered?'

'He was miles away, looking after Virgil Hardiman's cattle business,' the blonde responded. 'Twenty men will tell you as much if you ask them. It's all been checked out, Mr Stannard.' Her lips twisted into the faintest of sneers. 'It's as likely that you killed her as he did.'

'You're laughing at me, Alice Mears!' he accused.

'Perhaps you need laughing at,' the saloon woman retorted. 'You stand there like a latter day Moses on Mount Sinai! Don't take yourself so seriously, man! God didn't impose your mission.'

'Granted,' Stannard bit at her over the tip of his right shoulder. 'It's my brother's life that I take so seriously.'

'You're trying to pick up and return what he's thrown away,' the blonde advised. 'Let the damn fool hang. I've visited him in jail. He's a broken man. He wants to get it over with. He wants to die. Why don't you respect his wish?'

'You callous —!'

'Were you going to call me a bitch?' Alice Mears drawled amusedly.

'Yes, ma'am,' Stannard replied honestly.

'I've been called worse. Much worse.'

'You people of Shelbyville are so sure about everything,' he said, knowing that he had gone rather too far. 'Almost nothing in this world is as it seems.'

'So what do you think happened over at Merle's house that day?'

Stannard raised his eyebrows. Alice Mears was a direct woman – and she prided herself on it – but he hadn't expected a question from her that was quite so instantly demanding. Yet he tried to reply in exactly the same vein, telling her that he thought somebody unknown to the case could have entered Merle's hall just after Bill had left the house, seen her dazed condition, and perceived the chance to murder her in a situation that would almost certainly end in the crime being pinned on his brother. 'The killer would have had to be somebody who knew Bill and Merle's affairs well,' he concluded, 'and had much to gain from the deaths of both.'

'I'm sorry,' Alice Mears said dismissively. 'It all sounds very lame to me. Anybody going round to the back of Bill's house from the street would have been seen by folk passing there, and anybody entering his property from the waste ground would also have been under somebody's eye from one of the many surrounding windows. No, Mr Stannard, the jury was advised by the judge to avoid outlandish notions about what might have happened. Events, he said, usually occur in a natural and straightforward manner. Bill had what most folk regard as a strong motive for harming his wife, and the judge was satisfied that he had knocked her down the stairs and that she had died on striking the back of her head against a wooden table in the hall.' The woman released a heavy sigh. 'I can't spare you this. It must be said – because it needs saying. Your brother had gone down the hill in all sorts of ways before the murder, and he was no longer the high-minded and upstanding young fellow that he was when he first came to Shelbyville.'

Stannard felt his mood take another plunge. When derogatory things were said about another man, you could always dismiss them, but logical arguments usually isolated facts that needed looking at closely. First Iris Bates and now Alice Mears had spoken of Bill's moral deterioration in recent times. Any man who started drinking to relieve his personal problems did as a rule begin to fall apart. The need for alcoholic support denoted weakness of character. Booze had turned many a man into a monster. If he was honest in the matter, he didn't know enough about his brother's life in recent years to judge what the various stresses and strains in his business and love life had done to him. Bill could have developed flaws. Women were usually the first to spot the cracks opening in a man. Could it be that Iris Bates and Alice Mears were right on all counts? Had Bill in fact slain his wife and now deserved to die because of it? Stannard's faith was growing shaky. He could not dismiss the words of two intelligent females as being malicious and of no account. Where did the truth lie? His gaze was again fixed on that half dug well, yonder on the waste ground and not far from the back yard of his brother's home, and for a moment he wished himself at the bottom of it. Even though family bonds might be threatened, a man still had to do what was right. He was jaded by doubt and needed more time to think. 'Thank you, Miss Mears,' he said. 'I reckon I've done for now.'

'Have you so?' the woman said in some surprise. 'I had the feeling you had a whole list of questions lined up for me.'

'I've dried up,' he confessed.

'Well, you'll know where to come when you decide that I can be of further help.'

He nodded, feeling that in some indefinable way Alice Mears had defeated him, and knowing that he was close to the worst treachery of all, which was abandoning faith at the first real test of its strength.

'Why don't you go out through the kitchen?' the blonde suggested. 'You can avoid walking through the bar again if you do that.'

'To blazes with that,' he said sharply. 'I'm afraid of nobody in there, and I've done nothing to be ashamed of.'

'Suit yourself, Mr Stannard,' Alice Mears said.

Facing back into the room, Stannard made for the door opposite him and put his hand upon the knob. Then he checked abruptly, sensing movement on the other side of the woodwork.

'Is there something wrong?' the saloon woman asked.

'Does that fellow Manea always keep an ear to your door?' Stannard hazarded.

'Horry is no eavesdropper,' Alice said rather wearily. 'I set nobody to listen in.'

'Did you not?' Stannard growled, twisting the doorknob and opening up fast. 'I'd have sworn otherwise!'

He put his head out, but there was nobody to be seen – though he thought that he heard a door along the corridor to his right close hastily but with the gentlest of touches. Now Alice Mears was laughing to herself at him and, more annoyed than discomfited by her amusement, he didn't look back as he shut the door of her parlour behind him.

After that he headed for the bar-room and, after opening the door which separated it from the rear of the building, passed through and glanced at Manea's chair adjacent, seeing the spidery fellow coiled there as before and looking as if he hadn't moved since the first time that Stannard had stepped past him.

Oh, to hell with Alice Mears and her little games! Stannard felt more strongly than ever that the blonde had somehow beaten him all ends up.

FOUR

Emerging from the Gunpowder saloon, Stannard decided that lack of nourishment could be responsible for the decline in his spirits. He hadn't eaten in twenty-four hours and he needed a meal. Glancing down the street, he saw a sign that advertised Jade Doone's restaurant and, freeing his horse from the nearby hitching rail, he turned left and walked the creature towards the double glass windows of the eating place; then, securing his mount again, went into the establishment and sat down at one of the rear tables, ordering a large steak and vegetables, rice and baked apples, with a pot of coffee and milk cookies to round things off.

He ate everything put in front of him, and drank a quart of coffee – his mind at sixes and sevens amidst its various doubts and resentments – and his feelings of doom and defeat did decrease, but he could not fully regain his confidence in his brother's innocence and simply had to adopt a dogged determination to carry on with what he had started and not to expect too much inspiration from his shaken faith in another. The greatest men often proved to have feet of clay, and Bill was no great man – not when you got right down to it and stopped viewing him through the rose tints of brotherly love. He was at best determined, intelligent, and able; that cut above average. But no more.

Stannard built himself a cigarette and sat smoking it. His head ached, he felt lethargic, and he didn't know what he was going to do next. There was just one prompting in his brain, but it seemed too ridiculous to take seriously. He was still, mentally speaking, at the bottom of that incomplete well on the waste ground at the back of the Gunpowder saloon. Alice Mears had described his imaginings as 'lame', and his present idea could be one more feeble notion to put with the rest. Yet, if somebody had brained Merle Stannard with a brass candlestick, they would have needed a hiding place close by in which to get rid of the inevitably red-stained club. The well – wet or dry – was convenient to his brother Bill's back yard and, if the weapon envisaged had been used to crush Merle's skull, it could have been cast into the well in the hope that it would rest there unfound forever.

His cigarette largely burning away between his fingers, Stannard pondered the matter for several minutes; then, squashing out the butt of his smoke in an ashtray, he nodded decisively to himself. The matter was worth investigating – if only to eliminate the possibility – and, if by any remote chance the long shot should come off, it would tend to bear out Bill's story that he had departed from his home while Merle was still lying dazed but more or less uninjured on the hall floor, since it was unlikely that a man of his intelligence would have been fool enough to risk disposing of the murder weapon quite so close to home and under so many possible watching eyes from the houses overlooking the waste area that in some sense formed the heart of the town. True, it was also unlikely that, even if such a discovery should be made, the law would accept it in Bill's favour – for, at a pinch, he could have used the well as a hiding place as readily as anybody else – but a find of the sort would be a boost to his, Pete Stannard's, waning faith, and it was what he badly needed just now.

Summoning the waitress, Stannard paid his bill, and was making a small joke while he tipped the girl, when he became aware that somebody was peering in at him from the opposite side of the street. Alerting, he fixed the other instantly with his own stare, seeing a tall, narrow-shouldered, pock-marked man, somewhat pallid and nondescript of features, who was dressed in tailored garments that were now scuffed and frayed by much hard wear. The watcher had a cold eye that collided almost painfully with Stannard's own, and he jerked aside – as if suggesting that his apparent interest in the man at the restaurant table was accidental – then he moved off rapidly to his left, bent and vaguely furtive under his khaki Stetson, and he crossed the street and disappeared from Stannard's sight in a matter of moments.

Concluding his business in Jade Doone's restaurant, Stannard returned to the street, his quick eye seeking the vanished man again, but the other was nowhere in sight now – on either side of the road – and, giving the other what amounted to the benefit of the doubt, Stannard shrugged and went to his horse, taking his lariat off his saddle. Then, crossing the street with the rope hanging from his right hand, he entered an alley – which he judged to be a radial of the waste ground at Shelbyville's centre – and passed down the narrow walk until he emerged on the clayey flat where the unfinished well stood.

He aimed for the well, with its crumbling adobe top and safety covering of planks and, reaching it, immediately indicated his intentions to any watcher by shaking out his loop and attaching it to the heaviest of the planks lying across the mouth of the excavation, then throwing the length of the rope itself into the shaft below. After that he pushed aside the rest of the protective planks and seated himself on the well's parapet, his feet hanging into the depths; then, catching hold of the rope with the firmest of grips, he lowered himself hand-over-hand into the mud-scented gloom beneath and prayed that the well would prove neither too deep, foul, nor full of water, and his prayer was kindly answered on all counts, for the well was no more than twelve feet deep, entirely dry, and the air was as sweet as that above.

Standing on the bottom, Stannard let go of his rope and stood looking at the dim face of the chunked-out wall before him, letting his eyes accustom themselves to the sepia shades at the excavation's bottom, and presently he found that he could see well enough to take in most of the detail present. Not that there was much in the general sense to call his attention – for the original diggers had left nothing down here but broken flints and a lot of sand – and he was on the verge of accepting that he had got it all wrong and given himself a lot of hard exercise for nothing when, close to the foot of the wall on his right – and half concealed by the rut into which it had fallen – he made out an object that was of a handy size and obviously metallic.

Picking the shape up, he was momentarily inclined to laugh at himself – for he felt certain that he was only seeing what he wished to see – but he realised with something of a shock that his long-shot had paid off; for here, secure within his fingers, was what could only be the second candlestick from the pair that he had mooted would in the first place have graced the mantelpiece in his brother's kitchen. It was the sign that he had sought, and his faith in Bill's innocence immediately returned at full strength.

But the fact remained, nevertheless, that, significant though it might be on one level, the find proved nothing in the condemned man's favour and could even be made to worsen his case in the hands of a clever lawyer. Holding the candlestick waist-high in the surrounding shadows, Stannard rummaged out a match and thumbed it alight, using the glow of the flame in a close examination of the candlestick's base, and he saw clotted blood and brains which confirmed that it had been used in Merle's murder. Then, while still amazed by and thankful for his discovery, Stannard shook out his match and dropped the candlestick back into the same rut where he had found it, and after that he grabbed his dangling lasso again and began swarming upwards, the daylight soon whitening about him and the top of the well drawing close. Now he arrived at the limit of ascent and seated himself on the parapet again, recovering his breath in the personal certainty that his brother had been framed and that there was something behind this awful crime that was far bigger than the disaster which had overtaken Bill Stannard's marriage. Great evil invariably essayed great gain, as his mind had already softly prompted, and faint visions of what seemed barely possible were now trying to push through.

Spinning on his backside, Stannard raised his legs and swung them back over solid ground, staggering a trifle as he used his palms to thrust himself erect off the parapet; and it was probably that small stagger which saved his life, for a rifle banged from no great distance away to his right and lead ripped across the front of his shirt, burning the flesh of his chest beneath.

Dropping straight to his knees and claiming cover from the parapet of the well, Stannard snatched out his revolver and kept his head down in the expectation of more slugs flying in his direction, but no second shot followed the first and before long Stannard lifted his head the few inches that seemed wise and took in the full scene over to his right, his gaze picking up no movement on the waste ground itself or in the houses that enclosed the immediate semi-arc of it. But he did pick up a faint odour of drifting gunsmoke, and this aid to his senses focused his attention on the mouth of an alley that was almost directly opposite him. The shot that had come so near killing him had undoubtedly been triggered from that opening, and he was tempted to empty his revolver into the space, but he realised that his reaction would probably prove a waste of bullets and certainly call attention to him – which he wanted as little as the sharpshooter had; for his would-be killer had undoubtedly staked everything on the one shot, reckoning that a single explosion would do little more than raise a few eyebrows but bring nobody running, which would give him every chance to get away.

Stannard jacked himself upright. He listened hard, feeling the slight pressure of the breeze upon his face. From the main street came a clatter of hoofbeats and he felt sure that he was listening to the retreat of the man who had just tried to kill him. Clearly his presence in town had now been seriously noted, his words and activities reported to an unknown enemy, and this attempt on his life made as a consequence. So there could no longer be the smallest doubt that he had been interfering in matters that went far beyond Merle's death and the drama due to cost her husband's neck at noon on Saturday.

Then Stannard's thoughts went flying beyond the freeing influence of the immediate revelations. The shooting incident must be regarded as his link with everything hidden from him. It could prove a godsend, and it was up to him to make the best possible use of it. The sharpshooter was pursuable at this moment, perhaps catchable, and at least eventually trackable to the source from which he had come. That the projected bushwhacking had been organised here in town was also obvious – for the time element precluded anything else – but whether the gun had been hired or Stannard's attacker was his own man could only be determined by coming up with the man himself and getting his story out of him.

Ignoring the bullet-graze upon his chest, Stannard once more holstered his gun and willed himself to move, running back to the hitching rail outside Jade Doone's restaurant as fast as his legs would carry him. Freeing his horse, he stepped into his saddle and let fly with the rowels, heading for the western limits of the town at a pace that was truly reprehensible; but nobody called out or attempted to stop him and he was at full gallop as he cleared the built up area and went pounding out into the country beyond.

His heels working vigorously, Stannard permitted no let up. He kept his eyes fixed on the trail ahead and fairly ran his horse until its lungs roared and the sweat flew. This maximum effort was not enforced by negative feelings, but with a purpose, for Stannard believed that, once away from Shelbyville – and most likely believing himself unpursued – his quarry would slow up to save his horse and perhaps give his hunter the chance to bring him in sight. The reasoning was a little weak, but human nature had its common flaws, and a man with the audacity to undertake a drygulching in town must believe in his luck. That kind of belief could make a man slightly careless.

The trail ahead remained empty. Unable to understand it, since the distance and sheer pace at which he had travelled should have given him at least a glimpse of his quarry before now, Stannard swore to himself; but he knew the exact instant at which he had extracted the best from his horse and fetched the creature back to half pace. But still he journeyed on, lifting in his stirrups at intervals and peering all about him. In front of Stannard, wide and open, was a vast spread of country that lay green and mottled in the shadows of the mighty San Juan mountains. To the right, ridges fell back as steps, carrying green benchland high, while to his left a hogsback ran, grassed in places and riven here and there. Short of wearing a cloak of invisibility, no fugitive could ride unseen towards any compass point for long.

Now Stannard let go an angry sigh and settled firmly to rest in his saddle. He must accept the fact of it: he had lost his man. Was it possible that the other had back-tracked on him? Or that he had actually been riding in the wrong direction all along? A man in a state of shock could become disorientated. No, he couldn't accept that. He could trust his senses and knew what he was about. He had simply failed in his first test as a manhunter. Doubtless he was up against a professional and had made no allowances for the sharpshooter's wiles. This boded ill. One mistake was all it took, and he'd had his warning back at the unfinished well. A chill ran up and down his spine. If only he could keep heading into the west – but he could only do that by consigning brother Bill to the past. What was he thinking about again?

It was no good riding onwards like this. He was now simply travelling for the sake of it. Shelbyville was the site of his problems and back there he must go. Perhaps he would try to see Bill straightaway. It was five years since their hands had last touched, and that piece of time seemed to stretch into a small eternity now. Where was the sense in holding back? He could himself die before this day was out. No lawman had the power to deny visiting rights to relations of a condemned man, and he couldn't believe for a moment that the sheriff of Shelbyville would try it. Yes, he'd turn back now.

Stannard fetched his mount about. The land extended between him and Shelbyville like country that he had never seen before. But that, of course, was the common effect of a reversed scene, and he had passed through it, heading west, without absorbing much detail. It was really quite desolate – not unlike in atmosphere that cinder strip at the Chicago railroad station where Bill and he had parted, after the death of their parents from smallpox, to lead their own lives – and he was about to call on his horse to get them back among people again as quickly as possible, when he spotted riders up front and immediately drew rein in the shadow of a trailside rockpile, raising himself in his stirrups as he attempted to identify shapes that even at a distance of almost two miles seemed vaguely familiar.

Yes, the horsemen were three in number and there wasn't much doubt that they were Clifford Sandford and his two drinking companions from the Gunpowder saloon. The trio approached for about a hundred yards more, then turned left and began following a track across ground on which greasewood and sagebrush grew in abundance. They clearly had no idea that they were being watched and, for all that Sandford could easily have been the author of Stannard's recent troubles, were moving along in the relaxed fashion of men who had been enjoying themselves on their way home. And that would almost certainly be how it was. They were riding back to Virgil Hardiman's Toppling H which, if the signs were indeed correct, would be situated on the southern side of the hogsback that now traced the land as a dark and rearing line on the watcher's right.

Kneeing his horse into motion again, Stannard rode eastwards at a slow trot, keeping the trio under observation all the time and hoping that no head would be turned in his direction. His attempt at shadowing was not an accomplished one – perhaps because he was unsure that he had an adequate reason for snooping on the three men yonder in the present manner – but he was also wondering whether his original quarry could have galloped over the path that Sandford and company were using and passed into the shelter of the hogsback before he, Stannard, could have ridden far enough out of town to spot the movement. If that had been the case – and the logic and geography of the situation made an excellent argument for it – it would not be too much to place a question mark against the Toppling H ranch and ask if Sandford had in fact played the commissioning part in the bushwhacker's murder attempt. Now Stannard tapped a knuckle against his left temple, frowning his puzzlement. There had to be sense behind it all, but not too much was coming out of it as yet. He could only keep groping.

Stannard kept up his distinctly furtive ride and, coming to the spot where the sidetrail met the main one, he turned off southwards, now moving directly behind the three riders ahead. They jogged along much as before, without looking round or about them, and their obvious sense of security went on serving their follower well, since he was completely exposed and a single glance back would pick him up. But the trio were trotting closer and closer to the ridge all the time, and Stannard could now plainly make out the rift for which they were heading. Once they had entered that, he should be in no danger at all of being spotted, and he could then stir up his mount and put on a little extra pace. That much was obvious to him, but what he might see or meet on the further side of the hogsback remained a closed book that he somewhat feared to open. He knew that one person in the district wanted him dead, and there could be others too.

Now Sandford and his companions entered the cleft which they had been approaching, and a curve behind the great fracture carried them out of their shadower's sight. Stannard spurred to a canter, his mount trampling the sagebrush that intruded upon the track before them and raising a faint herbal scent, while the greasewood built small forests in the shadows round about and climbed right into the neck of the cleft. Echoes built and lifted, and high crags forced them back and down. Stannard rowelled his horse impatiently, and then they were into the gap – the way forming a fairly tight S immediately ahead – and, though he could see nothing of Sandford and company within these confines, he knew that he could not be far behind them now and might even be getting dangerously close.

Chancing it, Stannard slowed hardly at all and he traced the snaking pass without difficulty for a hundred yards or so, spotting its further end at a short distance from him as the way straightened. Still there was no sign of the trio that he had been pursuing, and that filled him with a kind of uneasiness – for the figures of his pace against theirs didn't quite add up any longer – but he suspected that the land beyond the egress before him fell away quite steeply, which meant that Sandford and the men with him could be less than two hundred yards ahead and hidden by the ground.

Reaching the end of the cleft, Stannard reined in and sat amidst the piled stone of a crumbling cliff that had been first shattered by earthquakes when the world was young. He gazed forward and down, seeing that he had been correct in supposing that the earth declined at the end of the pass, for a grassy slope dipped before him and joined a fine spread of prairie which rolled away to the lower edge of the southern sky and was blotched with herds that bespoke a ranching prosperity even beyond the normal for the lush plains of Colorado.

About half way down the slope, and calling Stannard's eyes in upon the movement itself, the riders of his earlier attention were making a slightly staggered descent among the boulders scattered before them; but then he realised, with a blurt of the deepest apprehension, that there were now only two present, which had to mean that one of them had separated from his companions while still in the great rift that split the hogsback at this point. The discovery ruined Stannard's appreciation of the magnificent ranch site which was also on view not half a mile beyond the point where the acclivity ahead flattened into cow pastures, and he wondered if there was still time to help himself.

He clapped a hand to his revolver, but in the same moment he heard the sounds of a repeating rifle being cocked and a man's voice said: 'It is you, by thunder! Cliff Sandford is sure going to be pleased about this. Get your paws aloft!'

Stannard raised his hands. He could well see how what his captor had just said might prove to be true.

FIVE

Slanting an eye over his right shoulder, Stannard watched the man with the rifle come surging out from between two rockheaps adjacent on a hammer-headed mount. The fellow had been the silent third man from the trio when the prisoner had first encountered them in the Gunpowder saloon. This third man now drew even with Stannard's horse and plucked the captive's revolver from its holster, shoving it into the top of his own trousers. 'Known as drawing your stinger,' he confided conversationally. 'Must say, you don't look stupid, but what else is anybody going to call you?'

'Smith, isn't it?' Stannard asked uncertainly.

'John Smith, yes,' the other acknowledged. 'What did you want to follow us for? Cliff Sandford had you under his eye from the moment you turned off the town trail.'

'That's interesting,' Stannard responded, just short of jocularly. 'Has he got eyes in the back of his head?

I'm damned if I saw him turn round and take a squint.'

'Naw,' Smith obliged, no less good-humouredly. 'Smart man, him. He carries a lady's hand mirror to do his lookin' back in.'

'I can believe he carries a lady's hand mirror,' Stannard said. 'I'd got him down as vain as a peacock.'

'You want to be careful what you say,' the man with the rifle warned. 'Sandford is a bad man to get the wrong side of.'

'I'm already on the wrong side of him, aren't I?'

'You sure are, Stannard.'

'What'll he do, Smith?' the prisoner inquired wryly. 'Will he gut-shoot me for trespassing? Any old excuse, hey?'

'You rode him hard, y'know. I do swear, mister, you gave him ten grey hairs he didn't have before.'

'What if it had been your brother that skunk was going on about?'

'A brother I ain't got,' Smith said unfeelingly, 'a sister I don't have, but a ma I've got someplace. My pa sort of came one night and went next morning.'

'Sounds to me like you're a proper bastard, my friend.'

'That I am, Stannard,' Smith agreed dryly, 'and it don't worry me a bit. One of those can get by as well as one o' them. Noticed?'

Stannard nodded, grinning. 'Why don't you let me

go, John? I don't have you pegged for a bad man. Why risk getting into a lot of trouble on Sandford's say-so? Just give me my Colt back and I'll mosey off.'

'There's some moseyin' to be done all right,' Smith acknowledged, the humour hardening suddenly at the back of the dark eyes in his lean, weathered face. 'I'm no more a dope than you are! We're goin' to mosey right down the slope under your snout and up to the first o' them buildings you see yonder. That's the ranch office, and where Cliff sitteth on the right hand.'

'He would, he would,' Stannard commented. 'I've no doubt that's where the privies are.'

Smith prodded the captive with the muzzle of his rifle. 'Giddup, smart ass!'

Stannard urged his horse forward and the creature picked its way daintily over a carpet of detritus and onto the slope beyond. He supposed he had earned the rebuke and should have known that it would prove a waste of time to attempt touching Smith's better nature. The man undoubtedly had his share of life's benefits to lose, and saints didn't wind up punching cows for their bread. Smith was just another employee, with an employee's mentality. He did his job, and there his responsibility in this world ended. If Cliff Sandford did something terrible to a prisoner down on the ranch, it would not be John Smith's concern. He'd have done his job, and a dead man more or less wouldn't matter much.

The horses went on plodding carefully downwards. Soon they reached the bottom of the slope. After that, Smith's rifle still at Stannard's back, they made for the ranch site, with its fine granite house and orchards in the background, corrals and stockyards at either end, barns, sheds, and bunkhouse patterning the middle area, and large wooden building closest to hand – which, from its draped windows and shining glass, also doubled as a home for the manager – that had a sign bearing the legend 'Toppling H Ranch Office' sitting astride its ridge.

Ignoring what might be coming next, Stannard took an interest in the place and would normally have enjoyed riding up to it, for he liked to judge the character of a master from the lay-out and cleanliness of his spread, but he was jolted out of his analytical thoughts when Smith suddenly pursed off a sharp whistle and the big-nosed, thick-shouldered figure of Bart Hengel almost immediately appeared at the ranch office door.

The foreman craned towards Smith and his charge; then, after calling a few words indoors, clumped down the steps that served the office building's verandah – Cliff Sandford now running out and hurrying behind him – and the pair of them simply halted on the grass and waited until the riders reached them. 'Did he give you any trouble, Smith?' Sandford demanded, eyeing the captive dangerously.

'He's got more sense than that, boss,' Smith replied

disdainfully. 'He's got a sassy tongue too. The idjit even tried to persuade me where my best interests lay.'

'Did he?' Sandford commented, feigning surprise. 'He's an idiot indeed. You already know that, don't you, Smith?'

'He's here, boss.'

Sandford gave his chin an emphatic jerk. 'Well, step down, both of you.'

Stannard swung to the ground in time with Smith and they stood facing the manager and his foreman. 'What are you doing on this ranch, Stannard?' Sandford asked hectoringly.

'I was shot at in town,' the prisoner said, seeing no reason to be other than completely honest in this matter, so far as it went, 'and I gave chase on horseback. The bushwhacker gave me the slip out here in the country, and I followed you here as much out of curiosity as anything else – though I reckon that guy who tried to kill me sloped off this way.'

'Be that as it may,' Sandford sniffed. 'So you followed us out of curiosity, eh? It was just curiosity?'

'Sure,' Stannard responded. 'I reckon I just wanted to see what was here to be seen. You know the feeling.'

'Somebody took a shot at him all right, Cliff,' Hengel observed, reaching out and plucking at the captive's bloody shirtfront. 'That slug wasn't far out.'

'Pity it didn't kill the nosey son-of-a-bitch!' Sandford ground out viciously. 'So you think whoever shot at you came this way, Stannard?'

'Figures so to me.'

'We saw nobody.'

'Wouldn't, would you?' Stannard sighed. 'Whatever the fact!'

'What was that meant to mean?' Sandford inquired, bristling.

'Here – or back in town,' Stannard explained. 'Been drinking, haven't you?'

'Are you again saying I'm drunk?' the manager snarled.

'It's all one, Sandford. You angered me while I was asking to see Alice Mears.'

'I loved your sister-in-law.'

'So I gathered!'

'There are no words in any language bad enough to describe that brother of yours,' the manager seethed. 'I wish they could hang him fifty times instead of once.'

'And you weren't somewhat to blame for whoring Merle?' Stannard bit in reply. 'I think you were – and you know you were!'

'Merle did what she liked, and so do I.'

'Great!' Stannard sneered. 'Now she's dead, and a man stands to hang. Sure, we're free to do as we like, Sandford – but we have to acknowledge the responsibility for what we do. You, and men like you, helped kill Merle, and may it haunt you in the small hours of the night to your dying day!'

Sandford whipped out his revolver. Thumbing back the weapon's hammer, he thrust the muzzle of the gun into the prisoner's face in the same manner as the barrel of Stannard's weapon had earlier been shoved into his own. Stannard could see that the manager was beside himself and in danger of triggering off, whether he meant to or not; so, reacting instinctively, he struck Sandford's right arm aside with his own left – the Colt thundering out beside his ear – then let go with a left hook that landed cleanly on the side of the manager's chin and stretched him on his back. For several moments Sandford lay there blinking, but all at once he scrambled up, still holding his gun and now spitting words of murder, and Stannard kicked the weapon out of his grasp and sent in a left to the solar plexus followed by a right uppercut, and down went the manager again, hurt and bleeding from the mouth but still fully conscious and glowering his will to give battle.

Stannard stepped back. All right; if Sandford wanted to fight, they'd do it properly. This time the manager came off the ground instantly. He released a straight punch at Stannard's head. Slipping the blow with total ease, Stannard gave his opponent two more to the jaw, staggering him, and had thoughts of driving the other's jawbone into his brain – for he could have beaten Sandford as often as the manager provoked it – when he was caught by the arms and pinioned, Bart Hengel hanging on to one side of him and John Smith the other.

Now Stannard struggled with the pair, sensing that their purpose was not to set him up as a target so much as to save their boss from further punishment, but it was never going to work like that, and Sandford plunged in with both fists flying and first doubled him forward and then began to batter him, the cumulative effect of the blows soon scrambling their recipient's brain and weakening his legs punch by punch, until they could no longer hold him up.

Stannard's knees buckled. Down he went on all fours bleeding from cut eyebrows, a squashed nose, and damaged gums.

But still Sandford went on hitting him, and would doubtless have kept it up until his victim had fully collapsed, prone and helpless; but, unaccustomed to the draining force of this violent exercise, the manager suddenly gasped and dropped his arms, admitting himself exhausted by expression rather than word, and he eventually nodded at Hengel and Smith – who were still standing by – and gulped out: 'Get him up! Get him into the office before I – I kill him!'

There was still pride in Stannard. He tried to rise of his own accord and, splay-footed, just about made it; but Hengel and Smith, obviously recognising his weakness, stepped in at once and now used the bracing power of their arms to keep him erect. Then, with him shambling between them, the two ranchmen guided Stannard up the steps that served the office building's verandah and then into the office itself, where they sat him down on a straightbacked chair against the wall to the left of the manager's desk and allowed him to slump forward and begin recovering himself as best he could. 'Well, mister, you weren't much to look at before,' Hengel observed unfeelingly, 'but there ain't a woman short o' desperation who'd look at you now. Boy, are you a mess!'

'He sure is,' Smith agreed. 'It'd take six doctors with a mile of catgut to put his face together again!'

'Don't exaggerate!' Sandford breathed, lurching to the back of his desk and flopping down in his own chair. 'That was barely a taste of what he deserved. He'll heal up – given time.'

'A month or so of it,' Hengel temporised. 'He sure ain't no advertisement for Hardiman's Toppling H right now, that's a sure moral. What d'you aim to do with him now, Cliff? Can we let him go back into town like that? We can't just kill him. He's now known hereabouts, and one or two of the hands witnessed the hiding you gave him. Could turn out tricky.'

'To the devil with the hands – and you as well!' Sandford flashed out waspishly. 'It's easy enough to justify what I gave him. He hit me first, he's proved himself a damned nuisance to everybody he's come into contact with, and he was trespassing – if not behaving suspiciously. Sheriff Joe Temple would rather a possible cow thief caught a beating than ended up dangling from a tree!'

'You encourage a thought there, boss,' the foreman reflected wickedly. 'Could be fixed.'

'Hey!' John Smith protested. 'Enough's enough, Bart!'

'You watch it, my man!' Hengel cautioned sullenly wagging a finger at his underling. 'It's your job to be useful – not start telling us!'

'There's no reason for this to go too far,' Sandford said judiciously. 'We're all sensible men.'

'Okay,' Hengel drawled. 'So do we put him on his horse and send him packing?'

Sandford gave his head the tiniest of reluctant jerks. 'If he'll give us his word not to head back into town.'

'There you are, Stannard,' Smith said, sounding relieved. 'You've got yourself a good deal. What could be fairer, hey? You gave Mr Sandford some grief, and now you've got it back.'

'Fine,' Stannard said flatly through his cut and swollen lips. 'Only I can't give any undertakings. My real business in this district is in Shelbyville.'

'You're talking "won't", you damned fool!' John Smith protested. 'There's no "can't" in this. Do you want to get done in?'

'The state of my face is my own affair,' Stannard replied, his words taking on a rubbery distortion. 'I'm not likely to talk about what happened to me on this ranch, am I? You've nothing to worry about. Unless there's something you want to hide and my doings might open up?'

'We've nothing to hide!' Sandford bellowed. 'Hint, hint, blasted hint! If you've got something special on your mind say it!'

'It occurs to me you could have murdered my sister-in-law!' Stannard responded no less aggressively. 'She'd dumped you for the mayor, hadn't she?'

'Are you – you out of your mind?' the ranch manager spluttered, gaping like a newly landed fish. 'Merle was the – the last person I'd ever have harmed. Her husband killed her. It's beyond all doubt! Merle lived dangerously, yes; but I – I didn't mind.'

'You just took advantage of her hot ass, eh?'

'There you go again!' Sandford stormed, clapping a hand to his holster and encountering only empty leather, since he had plainly left his pistol lying on the grass outside. 'Can't you believe any word I say?'

'It's a sorry business,' Stannard conceded, accepting that he had been harping to the detriment of everybody's intelligence. 'You're a nasty piece of work, Sandford, but I guess you weren't the only one. I just want you to grasp that a man is due to hang because you've no respect for the married state.'

'Respect – twaddle!' the manager jibed. 'You're hellbent on blaming everybody else for what your brother has done. If a man kills his wife, the blame is his and his alone!' He checked abruptly, and the bruises on his features stood out as purple blotches through the sweaty, waxen pallor of what was again his total fury. 'Stannard, you've pushed me too far. I'm not going to waste any more time on you. I'm going to – '

A big shadow filled the open doorway of the office – and all eyes turned towards it – while a man's deep voice boomed: 'You're going to do what, Clifford?'

Sandford sat up straight and drew in both hands under his breastbone, a look of mingled wariness and fear momentarily filling his eyes. 'Why – why,' he said haltingly, 'I – I intend to put this – this trespasser on his horse, Mr Hardiman, and run him off your property.'

Hardiman lugged the six-feet and two-hundred and fifty-odd pounds of his person into the office, his square face, with its high cheekbones and scimitar-shaped nose, expressing a kind of unspecified doubt and misgiving. Now, halting a pace beyond the threshold, he fixed the dark eyes under his heavily thatched brows on Stannard's battered features and breathed: 'God in heaven! Is that some of your work, Clifford?'

'He had to be taught!' Sandford declared self-righteously. 'We can't allow saddletramps to cross the Toppling H just as they like. Yes, I slapped the fellow around a little. He'll live!'

'Clifford,' the master of the ranch said scornfully, 'there are moments when I doubt that you have the right to live. Why didn't you simply take a club and smash the poor devil's face in? I'm ultimately responsible for everything that happens on the Toppling H, but it shames me to feel responsible for this. Trespassing? The man probably didn't even realise that he was on private property. The punishment you delivered went far beyond anything the offence could deserve. I'm disgusted with you!' He paused, his head shaking, but then his eyes suddenly narrowed thoughtfully: 'There's more to this than just a beating up, isn't there? I want to hear all about it. 'What's your name, boy?'

'Stannard, Mr Hardiman,' the prisoner replied. 'I'm Bill Stannard's brother!'

'So you're Bill's brother,' the rancher said, his manner losing its bleakness and severity. 'Well, I never! You must be Pete. Bill's my friend!'

'Bill *was* your friend,' Sandford reminded. 'He's dead now in all but the drop. Have you forgotten that he murdered your natural daughter? Yes, this is Bill Stannard's brother; but Pete is here to make trouble.'

'Trouble, no!' Stannard protested, realising that the mystery which had shamed the Bates family – according to Bill's letters – had just been explained to him. So the big rancher had once been the lover of Iris Bates's mother, and the dead Merle had been their daughter. 'I rode into Bill's tragedy quite innocently, Mr Hardiman. I rode into Shelbyville with the simple intention of visiting him; and not one thing more. I had been on the trail for weeks, and had no means of knowing about Merle's death and Bill's trial.' He touched the hurts on his face with quivering fingertips. 'I don't believe Bill's guilty of murder, and I want to make a try at proving his innocence. That offends Mr Sandford, and the violence between us has come out of that.'

'I don't doubt what you've told me is true, Pete,' Hardiman said, 'but you've certainly set yourself a task. I don't think Bill is guilty – I'd hold Merle's death against him far more harshly if I did – but the case against him does appear an unbreakable one. There may be much to unravel, but I don't see how it's to be done. All I can say is this: I have faith in God, and I don't believe He will let an innocent man hang.'

'I've said the same thing myself,' Stannard agreed. 'But God's miracles usually come by the hand of a man. We have to do the work.'

'Do you have anything new to go on?' Hardiman asked. 'I don't see how you should have, but – '

'Of course he doesn't!' Sandford interrupted. 'He's just putting his nose into everything!'

'I think the court misread the evidence,' Stannard said, pointedly ignoring the manager. 'Merle never broke her skull by hitting it against the leg of a table. Her head was smashed in by a blunt instrument. One that somebody struck her with. It's a brass candlestick, and I know where it's lying!'

'The hell you do!' Hardiman exclaimed. 'Where is it lying, boy? It could be reason enough for a stay of execution and re-examination of the evidence.'

'It's a yarn!' Sandford scoffed, waving the matter aside dismissively. 'He's trying to cobble together an impossible tale. He wants to confuse everybody. To get them believing they don't know what they believe. He's going to wind up in jail himself if he's not careful – for manufacturing evidence – and you'll find yourself with him too. He's trouble, Mr Hardiman. I've told you. Don't listen to another word!'

It was Virgil Hardiman's turn to ignore the manager. 'I asked you where, boy?'

'At the bottom of that half-dug well on the waste ground in the middle of Shelbyville.'

'I know it,' Hardiman said. 'So you found it and left it where it was?'

'Yes, there didn't seem much point bringing it up just then.'

'Any signs of the crime on it?' the rancher inquired. 'I suppose there must be.'

'It's still caked with dried blood,' Stannard replied.

'Would you be ready to go down and bring it up?'

'Sure – if it's still there.'

'I don't like the sound of that.'

'Well,' Stannard explained, 'while I reckon that candlestick's still lying where I found it, I'm sure whoever dropped it into the well knows I located it today.' He pointed to the bullet damage on his blood-stained shirtfront. 'I got shot at for my pains. I chased the bushwhacker out this way, after his attempt on my life, and lost him. I haven't the shadow of a notion who he is.'

'As to that,' Hardiman hazarded, 'I may be able to help you there. I found a dead man out on the range not an hour since. He'd been neatly shot. I heard the gun, and the noise drew me to where the killing had happened. I fetched the body in, and was on the brink of coming into the office about it, when this business we've been squabbling over checked me first.'

'Is the body outside?' Sandford queried.

'Bent over the man's own saddle,' the rancher answered, fixing his manager with an accusing eye. 'You know the hellion, Clifford.'

'What?' Stannard asked, just too quickly.

'Come and see for yourself,' Hardiman urged, snapping his fingers and including all present in the beckoning jerk of his head.

Stannard watched Hardiman turn away and step out of the office. The rancher was followed by Smith and Hengel. After that, looking as if he had the weight of the world upon his shoulders, Sandford rose from his chair and shuffled towards the verandah. Rising in a not so different fashion, Stannard tacked on behind the manager and walked back into the air, descending the verandah steps in Sandford's wake and joining the other men at the hitching area adjacent, where two more horses had lately been added to the number previously standing within it, one of them – a powerful but rather scruffy blue roan, with flea-bitten ears and a matted tail – carrying an unshrouded body draped over its saddle.

Winding his right hand into the deceased's scalplock, Hardiman turned up the almost featureless but pockmarked face of the dead man for all present to see and Sandford, glancing quickly at it, nodded and said: 'That's Eli Bazzarin, Mr Hardiman – as you very well know.'

Stannard jerked the dead man's Winchester out of its saddleboot and sniffed at the weapon's muzzle, the acrid stench of burned powder telling him that it had been fired not so long ago. 'Yes, this could have been the gun that damn nigh settled my hash. Who was Eli Bazzarin anyhow? I glimpsed that face in town.'

'Bazzarin was a professional killer,' Hardiman answered. 'For the right fee, he'd have shot his best friend, supposing he ever had one.'

Stannard murmured comprehendingly. There could be little doubt that this was the man who had tried to bushwhack him, and his knowledge had, therefore, taken another step in the right direction. Yet that was no indicator as to the identity of the person who had set the killer on; for that unknown individual had, on the obvious reasoning of it, most probably been the one who had shot the man to still his tongue about the deal. And that person was likewise now clearly emergent as the one who had slain Merle Stannard too.

SIX

Virgil Hardiman decided what was to happen next. He said that Stannard and he would ride into town, taking Eli Bazzarin's corpse with them, and visit the sheriff. From what the rancher could make out, it was time that Pete Stannard's new case concerning his brother Bill was put into the hands of the law. Perhaps the brain of a man paid to look into these matters would be able to penetrate where theirs could not. So, Stannard was sent to the crew's ablutions in the nearby bunkhouse and told to clean himself up – which he did as best he could – and when he returned to the ranch office he found the manager and Bart Hengel vanished away, while Hardiman and John Smith were waiting for him at the hitching rail, the latter standing by the roan horse with the body upon it, which had plainly been made his responsibility for the comparatively short journey into Shelbyville.

Hardiman looked Stannard up and down, and shook his head at what he saw; but there was no more talk, and the three men mounted up and left the Toppling H by the trail through the hogsback – each with a bowed head and immersed in his own thoughts – and they entered Shelbyville in what had become the evening light about three-quarters of an hour later, halting outside the sheriff's office as the man himself stepped out into the street and said: 'I saw you through the window, Mr Hardiman. Dead man?'

'Eli Bazzarin,' the rancher replied. 'Somebody killed him on my south graze – just off the trail that comes round into town from that direction. I heard the shot, and rode up shortly afterwards – to find him lying there, dead as you please.'

Sheriff Joe Temple, a tall man of athletic proportions, if ugly joints and tense, scowling features, went to the horse carrying the remains of the bushwhacker and examined the corpse with hands that were even rougher then Virgil Hardiman's had been in the similar circumstances back on the Toppling H. 'Good riddance to all vermin!' he spat. 'Whoever enticed this varmint into the district should be spreadeagled on a frame and horsewhipped! But that doesn't help, does it? I have to find out who did the shooting. Sounds to me like Bazzarin must have done a round trip of the Toppling H this afternoon – because he was in town at midday. I saw him boozing in Alice Mears' saloon. The two of them were cheek-by-jowl.'

'I wouldn't have put him down as Alice's ideal,'

Hardiman said sardonically. 'That's a girl who likes her men long, lean, handsome, and with something in their heads. But that's not important, Joe. There's a lot more to this than meets the eye.'

'There usually is,' the lawman acknowledged, lifting his gaze and considering Stannard critically. 'It has to do with you unless I miss my guess. You look as if you've been in the wars. If the gossip I've heard along the street is right, you're Bill Stannard's brother, aren't you?'

'I am.'

'Got involved in a piece of work with Cliff Sandford, didn't you?'

'I did.'

'Why the hell couldn't you stay away from Shelbyville?' Joe Temple inquired acidly. 'I've troubles enough this week without you adding to them.'

'Sorry,' Stannard responded woodenly, 'but I've got as much right in this place as anybody else. It's a free country, Sheriff. That's what the revolution was all about.'

'It's free,' Temple agreed significantly, 'while you behave yourself. Some of us have better judgement than others. We know how to leave well alone.'

'Ease off, Joe,' Hardiman pleaded. 'It's really his story that you need to hear. Stannard had been nominated Bazzarin's mark before Eli fell down on the job and his hirer turned him into buzzard bait on the strength of it. Or so it figures from where we stand!'

'Is that the way of it?' the sheriff demanded.

'I reckon that's the way it is,' Stannard replied.

Temple sighed resignedly. 'Sound off, mister. I'm listening. And don't spit and splutter. I can't abide it.'

Stannard shrugged. Once more he went over the hows and whys of his appearance in Shelbyville, recounted what he had heard from Iris Bates and Alice Mears – voiced his conclusions concerning his brother's trial and the finding of the brass candlestick at the bottom of the uncompleted well – and finally told of the bullet which had come so near killing him, of his chase after the drygulcher, his troubles on the Toppling H ranch, and how he had ridden in with Virgil Hardiman to put his discoveries and experiences into the hands of the law.

'Where they ought to have been hours ago,' the sheriff informed him bluntly.

'In proof of what?' Stannard asked, striving not to dislike the rather surly and bullying lawman. 'You'd have kicked me out of yonder door as a visitor with opinions he'd no right to.'

'I still may,' Temple gritted, studying the still mounted Stannard with an unyielding eye. 'But that's enough of that.'

'More than enough,' Stannard agreed. 'How about some action?'

Temple drew the Winchester rifle out of the dead man's saddleholster and sniffed at its muzzle.

'It's been fired,' Stannard assured him.

'So it has,' the sheriff said; 'but I wonder what that proves either?'

'I suggest we go and look for that candlestick,' Virgil Hardiman said. 'Stannard won't have enough light to go diving into the well if we leave it much longer.'

'I hear you,' the sheriff answered. 'Climb off those horses.'

'Me, too?' Smith asked.

'You get those remains to the undertaker, Smith,' the lawman returned, 'and my compliments to him.'

Smith touched his forelock. 'Yes, sir.' Then he fetched round both his own mount and the burdened horse, while his boss and Stannard swung down.

'Your party, Stannard,' the sheriff announced; and, chin jerking, Stannard led off in the wake of Smith and the retreating horses.

Presently the three men afoot turned into an alley on the left. They passed through the narrow walk between buildings and came out on the waste ground at the town's heart. Stannard placed the position of the unfinished well and headed towards it. Moments later the trio reached the adobe top work of the excavation and Stannard saw that his lariat was still looped to the same plank and hanging into the depths as before. Nothing appeared to have been disturbed up here, and he had little doubt that it would prove the same below.

Stannard sat down on the well's parapet again and let his feet hang into the shaft. Then he reached out and caught hold of the rope as before, lowering himself into space and descending with a sailor's agility. This belied the stinging pain which the exercise brought out of the shallow wound across his pectorals, but he ignored everything except his movements and touched bottom within seconds. Finding the candlestick didn't add up to much of a trick either, and he tucked it into his belt at the most comfortable angle that he could. After that, his nape prickling in the grave-like gloom which pressed in upon him at this hour of sunset and shadows, he seized the lariat and again went up it hand-over-hand, rising to the top of the well and swinging back into the company of the sheriff and Virgil Hardiman without pause. 'That's done,' he panted, noting now that the front of his shirt was wet from new bleeding

'You've got it?' the lawman asked.

Stannard removed the candlestick from his belt and gave it to Joe Temple, who held the base of the holder up to the glow still slanting in upon them over the rooftops to the west and used a thumbnail to scratch off a flake or two of the congealed blood which was visible upon the metal. 'Interesting gents,' he commented; then turned his eyes towards the back yard of Bill Stannard's not far distant home and pondered anew.

'I'm dead sure it's the partner of the candlestick standing on the mantelpiece in my brother's kitchen,' Stannard urged. 'I can get the key to the door from

Iris Bates, if you like, and we can go inside and compare the two.'

'Sounds okay,' the sheriff responded, 'but I can't really buy it. The crime may not have happened exactly as the court believed – and this thing could be the actual murder weapon but your brother could have come across here and thrown it into the well himself.'

'He'd have been taking one hell of a chance, wouldn't he?' Stannard asked a little angrily, for the sheriff had just stressed the big weakness that he had seen for himself in the story which he would like to attach to his find. He had hoped the lawman might be prepared to regard the flaw more tolerantly than he had been able to himself – or see everything in a rather different light – but that, of course, had always been a vain hope and he couldn't really blame Temple for being so annoyingly dismissive. He had been clutching at a straw, and straws always proved weak when required to carry any weight of logic. 'Does it make no difference at all, Sheriff?'

'The fact of it has to stand for something,' the lawman admitted. 'I can't just throw it up the corner and forget about it. I'll get on the telegraph to the U.S. marshal's office in Canon City. He can contact the trial judge; but I doubt if the find is big enough – in the circumstances – to warrant a stay of execution. It's no good me getting up your hopes for you, Stannard. I'd still be expecting your brother to die at noon on

Saturday.'

'The poor guy needs some comfort,' Stannard said unhappily. 'How if you let me sit with him for an hour, Temple?'

'I'd rather you didn't,' the sheriff returned. 'He's resigned, and as quiet as a guy ever gets when he's facing the rope. You'd be bound to raise some false hope in him. It's only natural when a fellow's had a day like yours.'

'All the same —'

'No,' Temple interrupted. 'Tell you what I'll do. I'll make you a deal. We'll keep quiet about your presence in Shelbyville over what's left of today and through tomorrow. Then if, as I fear, the worst comes to the worst – and I truly think it must, you know – I'll give you from nine o'clock until eleven with Bill on Saturday morning. You can jabber about a whole lifetime in two hours. How does that sound?'

'Pretty good,' Stannard admitted, acknowledging the sheriff's point. 'Two hours on Saturday morning could make it a little easier for him at that.'

'Somebody else murdered that natural daughter of mine, Sheriff,' Hardiman said grimly. 'Who?'

'You tell me,' Joe Temple countered. 'Bill Stannard's name is on the death warrant, and we've got a town filled with people who're satisfied he did it.' Then the lawman chuckled low and harshly. 'You stand there looking like the wrath of God, man! You do have ideas on the subject. Hell, I can see it!'

'Maybe so,' Hardiman said, surprising Stannard no less than he had surprised Temple.

'Go on,' the sheriff encouraged.

'It does me no credit to tell you,' the rancher finally choked out, 'but it's my guess Cliff Sandford brought Eli Bazzarin into these parts. I've half a notion he originally intended to employ that assassin to gun down Luke Warnes —'

'The mayor?' Temple once more cut in.

'It's straightforward enough,' Virgil Hardiman growled. 'Merle turned from Cliff to Luke, didn't she? I know Sandford was secretly as mad as a wet hen about it. Nor is he above hiring a gun. He did it once to see off a gang of rustlers.'

''That's mighty poor talk, Mr Hardiman, and it don't send you up far in my estimation.'

'I didn't learn about it until long afterwards,' the rancher protested. 'I wasn't best pleased – I can tell you.'

'If you feel about Cliff Sandford the way I think you do,' the sheriff said downright accusingly, 'why the devil don't you fire him? He's just another employee, when you get right down to it, and ranch managers aren't that hard to come by these days.'

'If that were only the whole of it!' Hardiman sighed. 'The fact is, Cliff has a hold of sorts over me. There's what you might call an ancient debt of gratitude hanging between us. Cliff's father was my best friend. Ivan Sandford set me up in business. He took no more than his money back, but he did request that I keep his son working as my manager in what amounted to perpetuity. I'm sort of stuck with Cliff. Nevertheless, if I could prove what I've just told you about Cliff and Eli Bazzarin, I'd get rid of him anyhow, but I have only my suspicions to go on – and they're not conclusive.'

'All a matter of proof, eh?' the sheriff said, seeming to crow a little. 'Now if that ain't the story of my life! Well, sir, Luke Barnes is still strutting around, and you've yet to tell me anything that truly counts.'

'Perhaps I can't after all,' Hardiman said. 'I suppose I've talked a bit and cleared my mind. It happens to me quite often. I can no more name somebody as Merle's possible killer than I can kick Cliff Sandford off my property. All I can say is – and it's on clear evidence that anybody may deduce – that somebody must have kept Bazzarin about here on a retainer, and that the person who dumped that candlestick in the well could have been somebody who regularly crossed that piece of waste ground and was a figure in whom nobody watching would have recognised any possibility of guilt.'

'Same person?' the sheriff demanded.

'It would fit.'

'Who?'

'No.'

'This is purely crazy!' Joe Temple exploded. 'You'd have done better to have kept your mouth shut, Mr Hardiman. All you've done is pile mystery on top of mystery where there's probably no mystery at all.'

'I'm sorry,' Hardiman said, his contrition undoubtedly genuine. 'I lost my inner vision, Sheriff.'

'If you say so,' Temple said shortly. 'Oh, to hell with this job! Are we going to spend all night here running on? Have you got anything further to say, Stannard?'

'Guess not,' Stannard answered, his mind probing hard at what Hardiman had just now said. 'All I want to do now is book in somewhere for a night's sleep. I didn't aim to close my eyes again until all this was over and done with, but I reckon we've come up against a wall right now. You're going to wire Canon City, Sheriff?'

'I said so, didn't I?'

'Yes, sir, you did.'

The lawman turned away and began striding through the swift falling dusk towards the alley by which he and his companions had earlier approached the waste ground. Stannard and Hardiman walked after him, and they regained the main street a minute later and made a right turn towards the law office. 'Stannard,' the rancher said, when they regained their mounts, 'you can come home with me. There are plenty of spare beds in my house. My housekeeper, Mrs Massey, will make you very comfortable.'

'You don't have to do that,' Stannard said, as the sheriff parted from them, entering his office with a curt 'goodnight' and shutting the door behind him.

'But I'd like to,' Hardiman replied. 'As I told you Bill

was my friend. We backed each other in Council affairs and had a lot in common. I liked the man. He was a good husband to Merle – who was after all my daughter – and he showed great kindness to her mother, Gloria Bates, before she died about a year ago. Seems to me, Pete, you too need a friend.'

'Reckon I do,' Stannard admitted, glad to fall in with the other – whatever the truth of his needs – since he felt the cattleman to be an ally who required his strength in matters that were important to them both but as yet obscure. 'I'll be glad to spend the night as your guest.'

'Good man.'

They climbed astride their mounts.

'What about John Smith?' Stannard inquired.

'I expect he's on his way home by now,' Hardiman answered, gigging up. 'Anyhow, he can look after himself. We'll go back by the south trail. The ride will take us near the spot where I found Eli Bazzarin's body.'

Stannard was in no sense thrilled by that prospect, but he passed no comment, since it was accepted that the older man was in charge. They rode slowly down the street, passing the cutback in which the newly built scaffold threw up its pale and ugly form against a black background, and soon they reached the town limits. Here they turned onto the south trail of which the rancher had spoken and spurred for a faster pace, while maintaining a silence which helped them concentrate on a path which was growing ever more obscure.

The sky filled with stars, and the wind boomed softly. Stannard felt the familiar freedom of the great spaces that fell towards the edges of the world. On their left the moon was coming up. Its rim was just riding the skyline, and the faintest of glows had begun creeping over the ground ahead of them. The light shimmered on the facets of bared flints and touched the shapes of prairie rodents that were fleeing their approach. Then the overlying hush was abruptly torn by the high-pitched yapping of a lovelorn coyote. But the quiet soon returned, and here was peace enough to cocoon the sleep of man and beast. Stannard, often a traveller in the dark, found it the stuff of dreams. It was good – utterly restful – and it made him wonder briefly how bad death could be. Yet death, it must be remembered, was the nothingness of night without end.

The thought shocked, and Stannard alerted sharply in body and mind. His spine magnetised, while his sixth sense came into play. He seemed to detect a presence lurking in their wake. A horse at the limit of hearing was being ridden in time with their own hoofbeats. Hardiman and he were being followed, and probably had been ever since leaving town. But by whom and for what purpose? Something new must be pending. He had felt that the day's events had worked themselves out, but perhaps the night was not to be a restful one after all. Maybe that unknown enemy was about to seize the initiative again. If it had ever been lost. You could be sure of nothing.

Then sounds that had been barely detectable became fully audible and vibrant – though the hoofbeats gave an impression of abruptly shifting through about twenty degrees northwards and magnifying out of a new start – and, drawing erect in his saddle, Stannard made a half turn at the waist and peered away to his right. 'There's somebody galloping to the north of us,' he called to Virgil Hardiman. 'Sounds to me like they're slanting for your ranch.'

'I hear them,' the cattleman replied. 'It may be John Smith. Maybe he paused in town for a drink or something. That man is a great one for leaving the trail and taking shortcuts.'

'I like the guy,' Stannard admitted. 'Cliff Sandford and Bart Hengel are what's wrong with him.'

'I fear so,' Hardiman agreed. 'They've got him jumping through a hoop. It's a pity he has no ambition.'

'Sure is,' Stannard said, suddenly dismissive, for it had just occurred to him that there could have been two riders in their immediate proximity and that the one who could still be clearly heard galloping on their right had simply come up fast out of the silence at their backs and the noise of his angling progress had swallowed the sounds of the one directly to their rear. The smudging effect thus achieved was now tending to suggest that the actual pursuer – who could have taken the opportunity to drop back a bit – had never been there, and that Stannard's ear had been the victim of an auditory illusion and never heard what it had seemed to hear in the first place. 'Did you hear the other rider behind us?' he now asked speculatively.

'No,' Hardiman said. 'Was there one?'

'I thought so.'

'Your ears are younger than mine,' the rancher conceded, hauling his mount to a halt. 'We can stop and listen.'

Stannard reined back likewise, and they sat rigid, listening intently at their backtrail – when not swearing softly at their horses – for the creatures, taken so abruptly out of stride, tossed and blew resentfully, making complete silence impossible to achieve.

'I hear nothing,' Hardiman finally said.

'Neither do I,' Stannard confessed. 'Perhaps my ear was in error. I make my share of mistakes.'

'You'd be an impossible fellow if you didn't,' the rancher consoled. 'What are we getting het up about anyway? We don't own the trails or the night. Other folk may be around and mean no threat to us. We're letting this thing get on top of us. How say you?'

'Reckon you're right,' Stannard said. 'I guess it comes of working up an atmosphere.'

'Let's ride on then,' Hardiman said. 'It won't be long before we turn on to my land. There's a marker in place.'

Once more they gigged up, and they had ridden less than a quarter of a mile further, when the marker mentioned by Hardiman appeared on their right. It took the form of a post that was around seven feet high and had the skull of what must have been an enormous longhorn steer fixed to the top of it. The presence was a weird one in the lunar glow – and a very daunting one too – but the master of the Toppling H ignored it altogether and Stannard gave it no more than a glance in passing, and they cantered onwards through the increasing spread of silvery light shed by the now steadily climbing moon – the rancher making his perhaps inevitable identification of the area in which he had picked up Eli Bazzarin's corpse – and presently they brought the lights of the ranch site in view and then passed through the herds which blotted the home grass and reached the house itself. After that they turned round the back of the dwelling and halted outside the kitchen door, where they dismounted and Hardiman said: 'My houseboy will have a bath waiting for me inside. If you'd like to use the crew's ablutions again, please do so. We'll have dinner when we've both washed off the dirt of travel.'

'Righto,' Stannard said; and the rancher left him and went indoors.

Now Stannard stood alone, reins in hand, and tiredly considered the dark and irregular shape of the ranch yard before him. The black outlines of several large buildings loomed nearby, walls picking up slight touches of the dull and oily lamplight which misted out of the bunkhouse windows and those in the manager's quarters at the back of the office structure beyond it, and Stannard was reflecting on how different everything seemed under moonlight and within altered perspectives, when he heard a rider coming up the northern end of the site and then made out the shapes of man and horse when the man reined in at the entrance to a corral, stepped down, and turned his horse into the enclosure, facing round with the task completed into a ray of light slanting out of one of the bunkhouse windows.

John Smith? So the man hadn't galloped back from town over the southern grass. Indeed it appeared that he had just come home through the pass in the hogsback which concluded the northern route. Well, that probably meant nothing in itself: though it did point up the question as to whom the horseman had been on the land back there closer to Shelbyville.

Now Smith vanished into the bunkhouse, and Stannard thought that he'd go and have a word with the man; but he had yet to take another step forward, when a door at the rear of the manager's living quarters opened a crack and light shafted out onto the ground opposite. Then part of a face pushed into view, the eyes peering furtively. Stannard watched intently. The person looking out was not Cliff Sandford, so it seemed probable that the ranch manager had had a visitor who was now departing – if a little too stealthily for the watcher's taste. In fact the process made Stannard wonder instinctively if any kind of honest business could have been transacted where such secrecy was present. He didn't believe so, for he was convinced that Sandford and crookedness went together like punishment and hellfire.

The door opened wider and a lank figure came sliding out into the night. Stannard saw at once that it was Horace Manea, Alice Mears' man from the Gunpowder saloon in town. John Smith's homecoming was unquestionably innocent, but Manea's presence was a quite different matter. There could be no need to look any further for the galloper on the southern grass. But what exactly could the spidery man have wanted on this ranch? And with Cliff Sandford, one of his employer's old lovers at that?

SEVEN

Stannard was tempted to go after Manea afoot – since he had a strong feeling that the man's presence on the Toppling H was somehow entangled with his own affairs – but he realised that to pursue the man in that blatant fashion would be unwise. Indeed, it would obviously be less than prudent to follow the man at all, yet Stannard felt a compulsion just then to leave no opportunity untested that might provide him with information that could help brother Bill.

Nor was this in any sense irrational or illogical; for, since leaving town, he had done some thinking about the possibilities which Virgil Hardiman had half evoked concerning Merle's killing and then withdrawn again as too uncertain to voice. The rancher had spoken of somebody who could have crossed the waste ground in Shelbyville without arousing much interest or suspicion – which had suggested, as another implicit factor, that the person in question could have been a regular visitor to Bill

Stannard's house.

When you came to think that matter over carefully, the person being mooted was an obvious one – again, Alice Mears, Horry Manea's employer. The woman's past involvement with Clifford Sandford had already come up more than once, and there was some cause for imagining that she had been the source of the retaining fee which had kept the late Eli Bazzarin – who could have been Sandford's original import – in the district. True, the reasoning did raise almost as many questions as it answered, but it undoubtedly provided reason enough for Stannard to want a serious talk with Manea.

His impulse suddenly becoming irresistible, Stannard remounted his horse and drew left, spurring off around the end of Hardiman's house by which he and the cattleman had recently approached the kitchen door. Under the moon, he put in a short gallop. This took him out into the home grass and along a wide curve to the east and west of the ranch site itself, an arc of interception that was more or less certain to cut whatever travel route Manea was likely to choose for his return ride to Shelbyville.

Stannard saw the man from town, already mounted and galloping hard, leaving the eastern side of the gap between the ranch office and the bunkhouse. Slowing, he interposed himself as exactly as possible on Manea's course. Calming himself, he prepared to make the interception as civil as the other would allow – for he saw no good reason why he need get into high words with the spidery man – but, while Manea could not have missed his presence and must already have spotted him in the moonlight on the grass, he was disconcerted by the fact that the other kept galloping straight at him and showed every sign of running him down if he didn't get out of the way. 'Hey,' Stannard yelled, holding his position in the night with a certain amount of stubborn courage. 'Hold up there, Manea, blast it! I want to have a word with you!'

But the plea implicit in this bawled request made no impression on the rider spurring towards him. Manea, now plainly deliberate in his blindness to reason and deafness to words, just kept charging onwards, and Stannard saw that the townsman could afford to, since he was seated on a horse that looked well nigh the size of a buffalo and appeared to be without a nerve in his body. The man had probably used these tactics before and found them absolutely effective. Anyway, everything about him warned that he wasn't going to ease off and, as the spidery man was already getting much too close for comfort, Stannard figured that he would just have to turn aside himself and let the townsman by. But it didn't quite work out, however, for his horse, already frightened by the possibility of a collision, responded too slowly to his pressure of heel and bit and, skittering into a low turn – when he required it to rear up and spin away –

failed to clear a path for the headlong approach of the other mount, and Manea's big horse hit Stannard's smaller one full on the left shoulder, literally brushing it aside. Over it went, and over went Stannard too, and he landed on his backside and then spreadeagled upon his shoulder-blades, conscious of Manea sweeping past, pistol out and thrusting downwards, and three shots boomed at him, the red flashes almost blinding, and he felt a tiny tremoring of the soil about his skull as lead drove into it, missing flesh and bone by only the tiniest of margins. Then, with an ugly shout, Manea was gone, his horse receding into the shadows south of the moon, while the night went on throbbing dully to the diminishing echoes of its hooves.

Unsure as to whether or not he had been injured, Stannard went on lying there for a minute longer. His horse, he saw thankfully, was already up, if clearly shaken, and he watched it trotting around in circles nearby, head tossing, nostrils blowing, and flanks pumping rapidly. Pretty sure by this time that he had sustained nothing worse than a few bruises and a severe shaking up of his vitals, Stannard struggled to his feet and beat at his garments. After that he lurched away to catch his horse – which he did without much difficulty – then spent a while talking to it to calm it down. That done, he took up the slack in his saddle-girths and climbed back gingerly into leather. Finally, with aspects of the petting still in progress, he drew the mount into a wide turn and encouraged it to make its way back into the ranch yard at its own pace, where he let it stand at the hitching rail for a few moments before stepping down again and securing it.

Now Stannard turned to the back door of the house adjacent. He had been conscious of light issuing from the kitchen from the instant of his return, and then a small movement drew his eye to Virgil Hardiman, who was standing outside and just to the right of the threshold. 'Where have you been?' the rancher asked. 'I heard shots.'

'It was Horry Manea,' Stannard explained – 'that guy from the Gunpowder saloon. He tried to blow my head off.'

'Manea was here?'

'I saw him come out of your manager's living quarters,' Stannard said, going on to give a full account of all that had occurred to him both here and out on the grass.

'Sounds like it's on again,' Hardiman said, a note of grim resignation in his voice. 'Pray God that's all there is to it.'

'How do you mean?' Stannard asked carefully, though he was sure that he had an at least vague and imperfect understanding of what the cattleman meant.

'Let's go inside,' Hardiman said, suiting action to his words and turning back into the kitchen – which he crossed with Stannard at his heels; and they passed through a door and into the hall, where they walked down the space towards the front of the house, turning left about half way along it and entering a well-lighted dining room that was furnished in a heavy but tasteful style and presided over by a rather plain, middle-aged woman who wore a bombazine dress and had the look of a chatelaine about her. 'This is Mrs Massey,' Hardiman introduced a trifle off-handedly. 'Get Chung Lee in here, Freda, and let's have some food.'

'Yes, sir.' The woman inclined her greying head over a pair of large and wrinkled hands which she held folded against her breastbone – very much the superior servant – and then left the room, the movement of her boots almost inaudible on the thick carpeting underfoot.

'Sit down, Pete,' the rancher said, indicating a place at the dining table which had been laid out with a spotless linen napkin, silver cutlery and crystal wine glasses.

Seating himself, Stannard was fully aware of the soiled and battered figure which he presented, but he did his best not to look too out of place in this rather sophisticated setting and sat in a relaxed fashion as Hardiman went to the head of the table and sat down also, picking up a long-necked bottle that had a foreign look about it and pouring wine into one of his glasses. 'French,' he said, passing the bottle down the table to his guest – 'from the Rhone valley. I import it at a ridiculous cost. Not bad; full of sunshine and fruit. But they produce stuff in California these days that's every bit as good.'

'At a fraction of the price?' Stannard asked amusedly, speaking a word of thanks but declining the wine, for he wished to keep a completely clear head. Then he thrust his feet out beneath the table and went on: 'I won't beat about the bush, Mr Hardiman. I think you were talking about Alice Mears when the sheriff got huffy after I'd been down the well.'

'Yes, I was,' the rancher admitted. 'Merle's best friend. There was a time when Alice was in and out of Merle's house all day long!'

'So nobody would have noticed her comings and goings all that much?'

'Just the point,' Hardiman acknowledged.

'I've been told that Alice had an affair of the heart with Cliff Sandford before my brother's wife entered the picture. Is that what you think is on again?'

'Seems so,' the cattleman said, savouring his wine. 'Horry Manea was their go-between before. He's a disgusting brute; always was. But he's never openly tried to kill anybody before. That I'm aware of anyway.'

'I got in his path.'

'And that's an excuse?'

'If my death is desired anyhow.'

'Yes – you could be a threat to somebody,' the

rancher mused. 'A mind coming in from the outside, eh?'

'A threat to Alice Mears maybe?' Stannard queried. 'My lighting on that brass candlestick would have been a rare facer to Alice if she dropped it in the well while passing between the back of Merle's house and the back of her saloon.'

'Again, just so.'

'If Eli Bazzarin was commissioned to send me kiting, then fouled up, Alice could have been the one to bushwhack him – in case I caught up with the varmint and beat the truth out of him. It was also a fact that I had glimpsed Bazzarin's face in town, and he could have mentioned it to her.'

'It all fits, doesn't it?' Hardiman agreed.

'Girls of easy virtue usually share their men with indifference,' Stannard calculated. 'Alice could have made it appear like that between Merle and her – where Sandford was concerned – but she could have felt a lot angrier about it than she let others know. Including Merle. Women are queer cattle when it comes to things like that.'

'Damn right,' Hardiman conceded, pouring himself a second glass of wine. 'And the best way to get a fellow back is to do him a big service while you're about it.'

'Now you have lost me,' Stannard confessed.

Just then a Chinese male of indeterminate years entered the room, the seamed yellow of his curiously pleasing features a wreath of smiles, and the white jacket and black trousers of his western servant's attire newly pressed and spotless. He carried before him a large tray with a cover upon it, and over this he bowed to the master of the house before setting it down at the centre of the table. After that he removed the top from the tray, revealing the dishes of fare upon it, and then he served Hardiman and Stannard with lamb cutlets, new potatoes, peas and asparagus, an infusion of mint bringing its special fragrance to the whole table. 'Thank you, Chung Lee,' the rancher said. 'Eat up, Pete. No ceremony here, boy. I ate at a thousand campfires, and nothing in this world tastes better than a fat trout grilled on a stick over a pinewood fire.'

'My sentiments too,' Stannard chuckled, pitching in with gusto and holding back from the smallest hint that Hardiman should go on explaining his mind while the meal was in progress. There were matters of etiquette and decorum – not to mention digestion – which he, too, had learned.

Hardiman, however, showed complete indifference to the conventions of the meal table and promptly went on: 'It was always plain to me that that daughter of mine and Alice Mears knew more or less everything about each other's business. When Cliff Sandford became Merle's lover – and much too familiar and demanding with me on that account – I made up my mind that it was time to split them up if I could, as much for Bill's sake as my own. So I decided that, on my death, Merle should have not only my money but the ranch itself, which I had already told Cliff was down in my Will for —'

'He was after all the son of the best friend who had set you up in business,' Stannard sympathised judiciously when the other broke off.

'Even so,' Hardiman said heavily, 'such a gift went far beyond the obligation incurred and, in the circumstances, I felt justified in changing my Will to fight the present wrong in the best way I could. So I met Merle and informed her of what I meant to do – though in fact I never did do it, out of my continuing sense of gratitude to Cliff's father – knowing that she would tell Alice Mears and that Alice would pass it back to Cliff. That, of course, was exactly what did happen, and it led to a rare old bust up between Merle and Sandford – both of whom were jealous of their positions in my life and constantly believed I was favouring one ahead of the other. It was then that Merle turned to Mayor Luke Barnes, and Sandford, realising what he had lost, I suppose, started doing all in his power to get Merle back. It's a bit messy and none too clear-cut, but young Merle went on in her new adulterous relationship, and that was that. Until —'

'She was found dead,' Stannard resumed. 'So, with Merle dead – presumably at her husband's hand – Sandford could once more regard himself as your heir?'

'If tentatively,' Hardiman agreed meaningfully, 'since I was careful not to amend the matter by word or deed.'

'Were you afraid of a bullet if you did?' Stannard hazarded. 'Was it your notion that Alice Mears was keeping Eli Bazzarin around on a retaining fee to put a bullet in to you as soon as she was sure that Sandford was back in your Will?'

'It was something I felt more than reasoned,' Virgil Hardiman admitted. 'If I'm anywhere near the truth – and I've a feeling deep in my guts that I am – Alice Mears deliberately saved Cliff from himself by killing Merle and so eliminating the need for Sandford to use Eli Bazzarin to bushwhack Luke Warnes, an obvious crime to those in the know. Yes, there was probably a conflict of motives present at the start, but I see Alice as the brain and driving force behind all that's happened, and Cliff may have been to some extent forced to go along with her. Circumstances have their power, Pete, and Cliff Sandford is a weak and greedy man who would be prepared to let a woman show him the way to what he wants.'

'What she wants too,' Stannard said to his dinner plate, thinking of how the Mears woman must have exploited the bad blood between Bill and Cliff Stannard in order to murder the one and bear lethal false witness against the other in a court of law. 'I'd like to know what Horace Manea was here for tonight.

I'm certain he wasn't delivering a billet-doux. What did Sandford go to town for today? Was he simply on the booze?'

'No, he was there on ranch business,' Hardiman answered. 'He had a meeting with Wendell Sligo, our lawyer. It had to do with a beef contract on which we'd been incorrectly paid by a firm of Chicago butchers.'

'Is Wendell Sligo also your personal lawyer?' Stannard inquired.

'He's the only lawyer in town. He handles everything.'

'Then a copy of your Will is in his possession?'

'I hope I'm misunderstanding you,' the rancher said, looking up sharply.

'No, you're not,' Stannard assured him. 'How far can you trust that man Sligo?'

'About as far as you can trust most lawyers.'

'That being the case,' Stannard said, smiling cynically, 'Sandford probably knows what's in your Will and could have done all along.'

'Which suggests I'm in danger right now?'

'Could be.'

'Accepting you're right, Pete, why have they held their hand this long?'

'Maybe they want to see my brother dead and buried first,' Stannard prompted. 'Perhaps they haven't wanted to risk anybody trying to connect your sudden death with the Bill and Merle Stannard affair.'

'But who could do that?'

'Mayor Luke Warnes?' Stannard wondered. 'I don't know the man, but he might. He must have influence too.'

'I just can't see it,' Hardiman said. 'Luke Warnes isn't the brightest man around, and he wouldn't look beyond Merle. Unless he had a mighty good reason.'

'It's possible Sandford and Alice Mears are afraid of something Merle could have said.'

'No,' the rancher responded fairly emphatically, shaking his head. 'They'd go on being afraid, and it's likely something would have been said by Warnes before now.' He repeated both the negative and the shake of his head; then shouted: 'You lurking, Chung Lee? Let's have some apricot pie in here!'

At that moment a window flew to bits at Hardiman's back and Stannard heard the crack of a shot from somewhere not too far away outside. In the same instant the rancher uttered a choked cry and sprawled forward on the table, the right-hand side of his skull apparently torn open and blood streaming everywhere. He looked a dead man, and Stannard didn't doubt that he was.

EIGHT

Leaping up from his chair, Stannard hesitated between the shot man and the shattered window; then, figuring that he could do nothing for Hardiman but might have some chance of catching the killer, flew to the window. Freeing the latch, he threw the frame itself wide open and, bounding on to the sill before him, ducked through the window-space itself and dropped to the ground about four feet beneath.

Sinking over his knees, he used the muscles of his thighs like springs and came up fast, launching himself into a run and making for a spot about fifty yards away where in the moonlight he could see a figure trying to climb astride a horse. It was a case of more haste less speed, and the other was dragging along from the stirrup and failing to rise. Increasingly baffled by the ineptness of its rider, the mount grew agitated and began to prance and sidle, while the person trying to lift into the saddle tugged its head in the opposite direction and made a fight of it where co-operation was needed. It was all rather a shambles to witness – and could have ended with the horse breaking free and running wild – but desperation helped the rider hang on and finally swing up, split-legged, into a seat of sorts. But even then the mount was far from under full control and refused to square up and loose out into a gallop.

Stannard's legs scissored at the speed of a youth's. He found himself approaching the bushwhacker much faster than he had believed possible. Suddenly he realised that he was within ten feet of the now clearly panicking fugitive, and he propelled himself into a huge jump. His leap was true, and his hands were about to land on a pair of slight shoulders, when an elbow swung back at him and hit him in the centre of his face. This diverted his grab the inches necessary to render it abortive, while the rider flattened towards the animal's neck and rowelled it cruelly. The horse then knocked the reeling Stannard further aside with a blow from its left flank and, as he tumbled to his knees, it went off at full speed, haunches surging and its front hooves barely touching the ground during the first steps of its flight.

'G'dammit, I know it's you, Alice Mears!' Stannard shouted after the fugitive, his rage and frustration getting the better of him as he scrambled to his feet. Then he reached for his holster, intending to scare the woman with a few bullets fired round and about her, but only intensified his chagrin when he realised – though not for the first time – that he had failed to recover his Colt from John Smith after the events that had followed his capture on the hogsback.

With new blood flowing from his nose, he cursed himself roundly for the oversight. After that he let the curse grow and cover a still greater anger with himself. For he now saw clearly why he had felt that Virgil Hardiman's life was in danger while they had been talking together before the fatal shot had come in through the window. Some part of his mind had been foreshadowing the bullet, yet he had failed to realise consciously that he had feared this because Alice Mears could so easily have seen him on the waste ground behind her saloon with Hardiman and the sheriff that evening and instantly recognised that the rancher could tell him about the Hardiman Will and the money and property matters which had bracketed Merle, Stannard and Cliff Sandford. Nor could there any longer be any doubt that Stannard's ears had been in perfectly good condition when he had believed that he had heard that first horse behind Virgil Hardiman and himself while they had been riding back from Shelbyville. It had been Alice Mears dogging them all right; and that made him realise what a curious instrument the mind was. It was capable of both wonderful inspirations and times of inexplicable weakness. But it was no good bewailing what had caused his recent mental blindness. Done was done. Virgil Hardiman was lying back there with a bullet in his head and, while the rancher's murder could be avenged, the only practical service a friend could offer him tonight would be that of digging his grave.

Setting his arms akimbo, Stannard spent a minute staring into the wake of the now far departed Alice Mears – wondering what in tarnation he could do about proving her crimes now that Virgil Hardiman, who alone could have confirmed so much of the background detail which pointed up her wrong-doing, had taken the ferry – and then he flung away, kicking angrily at a tussock, and strode back in the direction of the ranch house, climbing back indoors when he got there through the window space which had been left gaping when he had leapt out to begin chasing the bushwhacker.

Virgil Hardiman was still sprawled forward on the dining table, as he had been when Stannard had last seen him, and the blood was still running from his head and dripping to the floor off the edges of the table. Chung Lee, the Chinese houseboy, and Mrs Massey, the housekeeper, were both standing just inside the door that gave access to the hall – one to the left and the other to the right – while between them, but still out in the space beyond, stood Clifford Sandford, his shoulders hunched into a camel hair dressing-gown and his hands lost in the deep pockets at the front of the garment. His cheeks wore a faint pallor and his lips were firmly compressed, but his face was otherwise expressionless. Indeed, the man's demeanour was such that it brought Stannard's temper flaring out again 'Damn your eyes,' he seethed, 'and may you burn in hellfire!'

'What – what's that for?' Sandford spluttered.

'You know what it's for!' Stannard returned, standing in front of the room's broken window and pointing at Hardiman's body. 'Alice Mears did that!'

'You're out of your mind!' Sandford fired back scornfully. 'What – what proof do we have that – that you didn't do this?'

'I was eating dinner with the man!' Stannard snarled in reply. 'Any fool can see that he was shot from the ground outside!'

'So you say.'

'I suppose Horry Manea came here tonight to warn you of what Alice Mears was planning to do, Sandford?' Stannard gritted. 'I can just see it. That woman knows what a weak cent's-worth you are! She'd know you had to be prepared for it – so's you didn't mess up anyhow when it happened.'

'Horry Manea was – wasn't – ' Sandford protested, floundering to a stop.

'Wasn't here?' Stannard completed for him, the scorn now thickening his own voice. 'Oh, yes, he was, mister! I saw the man with my own eyes, sneaking out of your back door, and then he bolted so fast he charged my horse over with his own. He also tried to kill me with his gun. He was here all right!'

'Go tell your lies to the sheriff!' Sandford advised

coldly. 'He may listen, but that's all he's likely to do. Ever hear of proof?'

'There's plenty of that around,' Stannard bluffed. 'Enough to hang the pair of you!'

'I wasn't born yesterday,' Sandford sighed. 'Everybody for miles knows that Alice and I are more than just good friends. They may have a dirty snigger about it, but that's a long way short of believing us partners in anything shady. Nor was Virgil Hardiman the best loved of men. Far from it. He was a sight too successful to begin with, and much too outspoken for the general run of people. He was a hard man, and always gave a Roland for an Oliver.'

'A hard man but a fair, I'd judge him,' Stannard said, 'and that's the best kind to be. Folk know where they are with such. He will always make enemies, but will never take unfair advantage of them. He was your father's friend, Sandford, and not by accident. I'm dead certain he's been yours too. If your pa were around today, I figure he'd stand you out to scare crows, because that's all you're fit for!'

'Well, he isn't, is he?' Sandford responded disdainfully. 'Keep it up, Stannard! The acid in a man like you finally eats his own guts out!'

Stannard drew the deepest of breaths and held it. 'Wasn't that the truth, though? He had often seen it for himself. Hatred – even hatred of wickedness – always, by this road or that, killed the hater. Emptying his lungs, he filled them again, striving for a measure of calm, and he found it on looking at Chung Lee and Mrs Massey. It was clear that neither servant had any idea of what he had been talking about, and that both were becoming scared of him. This exercising of enmity was doing no good. Sandford was known here, whatever his failings, and he no doubt enjoyed a certain amount of respect; but he, Stannard, was a stranger and inevitably on sufferance. There were practical things that needed doing here, but when you had no authority of your own, you had to work through somebody else's. 'Truce, Sandford,' he said. 'Mr Hardiman will have to be moved. I need help to get him away from the table. Is it to be you – or another?'

'Stannard, I wouldn't do a hand's turn to help you,' the manager announced bluntly. 'I'll walk down to the bunkhouse and send John Smith up here.'

'Okay,' Stannard said. 'Please ask Smith to bring my pistol with him.'

'I'm not so sure that I'm going to let you carry a firearm on this ranch,' Sandford said. 'I'm the only boss on the Toppling H now.'

'Suit yourself,' Stannard replied shortly. 'This is work that has to be done.'

The manager appeared to make a tacit acceptance of that. 'Are you going to take him upstairs to his room?'

'Is there any need for that?' Stannard wondered. 'If we take him up there, he'll only have to come down again. And he's a rare size! Best show some consideration for the undertaker's men.'

'I'll go into town and make the arrangements first thing,' Sandford said. 'He's always wanted an oak coffin and brass fittings.'

At those words, Mrs Massey seemed to grasp the full enormity of what had happened and burst into tears. She ran out of the room and, after a moment's hesitation, Chung Lee followed her, his own expression utterly woebegone.

'Servants,' Sandford sneered.

'Perhaps they loved their master more than you did,' Stannard suggested.

Sandford scowled at his slippered feet and made to turn away.

'Oughtn't you to call the sheriff in?' Stannard added quickly.

'It'll do in the morning,' the manager said querulously. 'What is there that can't wait until the morning? There's nothing anybody can do about any of it tonight.'

It was not the correct move, and Stannard knew why Cliff Sandford was practising delay. The murder of Virgil Hardiman had not gone quite according to plan. It had gone awry in that Stannard had seen enough of the killer to be able to name her as Alice Mears, and this meant that direct denial of the crime was the only course open to the saloon woman now. If Sandford had been in a situation that rendered him some latitude before, he must now be asking himself whether he any longer had any choice but to back her to the hilt whatever happened tomorrow. If he rode off while the chance was still there – which was probably the wisest move he could make – he would have to leave the Toppling H behind for good and lose everything. He would not do that. Stannard was sure that the man's greed was greater than his fear. No, it was going to be a game of outright bluff for him and Alice Mears from now onwards; but, given they kept their nerves, they'd most likely pull it off because it would work out as their word against Stannard's, while the actual evidence involved remained of the speculative and circumstantial kind. Basically, the ranch manager was seeking time to think right now and get a clear picture of the pitfalls that could lie ahead. 'Don't blame me if the sheriff cuts up rough with you over the delay,' Stannard warned in a casual aside.

But the lingering Sandford ignored the words, and now moved away from the dining room door and vanished into the back of the house.

Left alone with Virgil Hardiman's remains, Stannard began clearing the dishes, cutlery, and glasses from the table and putting them on a serving trolley that stood to one side. That done, he carefully lifted the rancher's torso from the back of the shoulders and sat Hardiman upright in his chair. After that he pulled the cloth off the table and cast it to the floor, intending to use it as a shroud in due course, and about then John Smith entered the room, holding Stannard's Colt by the barrel and offering it to its owner.

'So Sandford let you bring it to me,' Stannard said, taking the weapon from the other and thrusting it into his holster.

'No, my idea,' Smith said shortly.

'Obliged anyhow,' Stannard said, eyeing the ranch hand carefully. 'I've missed that gun, and had need of it.'

'What the hell has been happening around here tonight?' Smith demanded, shaking his head over Hardiman's body. 'Who'd want to do a thing like that?'

'If you don't know,' Stannard replied, feeling Smith to be both a wavering enemy and an uncertain friend, 'I'm hardly the man to enlighten you. All I can say is, you're keeping bad company, boy, and it's getting worse all the time. If I were you, John, I'd haul my freight. You may figure you've got preferment on this place, but I don't reckon it's going to last a lot longer. You could still have to put down a high price – your life even – and thus come up with nothing.'

'Riddles, Stannard?'

'No, just Sandford and Alice Mears,' Stannard answered. 'Hell, man! You must have some idea what that evil pair are about!'

'I work here,' Smith said, looking and sounding

rather stubborn, 'and that's all. I was ordered up to the house to help you. What do you want me to do?'

'I want you to help me get Mr Hardiman out of his chair,' Stannard responded. 'He can lie on the carpet in front of the fireplace. That should make it easier for the undertaker, when he comes in.'

'Okay,' Smith said, gripping the back of the chair that held the dead man and tipping it towards him until he was able to twist the piece of furniture as a whole with force enough to face the hearth. After that he rested a moment, then went on: 'If we lift the body out as it sits, then set it down and flatten it, we should have the job done.'

'You've solved it, mister,' Stannard approved.

Closing on the front of the chair, they did what Smith had suggested – employing more muscle than reverence because there was no other way – and, once they had the body lying on its back with the limbs straightened, Stannard picked up the tablecloth again and shrouded the remains. 'It was a bigger job than I could have managed alone,' he said. 'Thanks, John.'

'All part of earning a living,' Smith replied. 'Look here, Stannard, I'll bear in mind what you said to me.'

'You're a free agent, man.'

Smith smiled crookedly, mixing doubt with bleak humour. 'Anything else you want before I go?'

'Don't see what,' Stannard said.

'I'll go back to the bunkhouse then.'

'If it doesn't sound like an hypocrisy – goodnight.'

'Goodnight.'

Stannard watched the ranch hand step out of the room and face right in the hall. Then he listened as the man's footsteps receded in the direction of the kitchen and soon faded out completely. He had offered Smith what guidance he could – perhaps gratuitously – and the fellow must now make his own decisions. Dominated by manager and foreman as he was, the guy could again turn up as an enemy before the night was over – since Stannard realised that his own position on the Toppling H was an ambiguous one at present to say the least of it – and Sandford could still decide that he was too much of a threat to leave running around loose and take some drastic action to seal his lips. The danger was plainly there, and the risks that lurked around it were also clear, but he could only go on as he had been going for moment and see if anything untoward did develop during the night. Most likely nothing would, for the ranch manager might well conclude that he would be wise to eschew all kinds of violence for the present. Those forced to rely on bluff must do all in their power to avoid their bluff being called.

Squaring his shoulders, Stannard reckoned that he would go and find Mrs Massey. That bed which he had been promised must still be available. He could at least make himself comfortable while waiting to see whether or not anything of a threatening kind did manifest before dawn. Whatever happened, he would be better off than the poor devil lying on the carpet beside him, and he glanced down regretfully for what he intended to be the last time before heading for the hall, but what he saw gave him a nasty shock and seemed to freeze him to the spot, for there was a stirring under the tablecloth and a truly sepulchral groan rose with it, the sound filling the heavy silence of the room with an eerie thrill.

Reaching down, Stannard snatched the tablecloth off the rancher's body. He saw at once that Hardiman's chest was rising and falling, and that the hands resting on his abdomen were full of a convulsive twitching. Short of being dead, the cattleman now appeared to be very much alive – if emerging from a spell of deep unconsciousness – and, moving to the other side of Hardiman's head, Stannard knelt down and studied the wound there with a care that nobody had exercised before this. Now he slowly realised that the bullet from the killer's rifle had not actually penetrated the rancher's skull at all but had simply skidded around it, following the bone structure itself and tearing away a large enough quantity of flesh and hair to cause heavy bleeding and create the impression of a terrible hole where none in fact existed. The impact had plunged Virgil Hardiman into a state that had looked like death, yet in reality he was not too badly hurt. With luck, he would be himself again before the night was over. A man of bull-like proportions, he obviously had the thickness of skull to match the rest of his skeleton.

Sitting back on his heels, Stannard made no effort to check the sudden racing of his brain. The discovery that the rancher was still alive must change everything radically, for new conclusions were now possible. Sandford and Alice Mears could once more be confronted with confirmation of the monetary and financial machinations which Hardiman had undertaken in the background of his illegitimate daughter's life, and the reason for Alice Mears' attempt on his life would become both obvious and irrefutable. What was more, the cattleman would only have to speak up and his, Stannard's, evidence, including that of the brass candlestick, would be worth consideration by the lawyers who had been originally involved in brother Pete's murder trial. The pattern of crime was there, and it only needed firming up by Virgil Hardiman's testimony to stand a good chance of freeing Pete and taking the threat of the rope elsewhere. But – what if Hardiman were attacked again before the law could benefit from all he had to say? Once it was known outside that he had in fact survived the bushwhacker's slug, the word would travel like wildfire the district over and, alerted, the enemy would redouble their efforts to silence the rancher forever. Therefore, difficult as it was going to be, the fact of Hardiman's survival would have to be concealed for the time being – tonight at the very least.

Stannard walked quietly over to the door and closed it with the softest of clicks. Then he stood behind the woodwork and searched his mind for magical tricks or effective ruses, but he found neither in his mental armoury. When a man got right down to it, just about everything in this life had to be done the hard way. In order to hide Virgil Hardiman, he would have to get the rancher to a hiding place without anybody seeing what he did. That also meant persuading the man involved that what he was doing was necessary. His arguments would have to be good, and he must somehow win the immediate silence of a perhaps badly dazed man who might soon be demanding all kinds of attention from everybody on his payroll. It was a tall order, and perhaps an impossible one, but he could only try to carry it out. The key to success was there and nowhere else.

On the nearby serving trolley stood a jug of water which Stannard had recently placed upon it while clearing the dinner table. Walking to the trolley, he picked up the jug and carried it over to where the still no more than stirring Hardiman lay. Kneeling again beside the rancher's head, Stannard removed his own neckerchief and soaked the cloth in the water, laving Hardiman's face and wound after that with the lightest movements that he could manage. Perhaps two minutes went by, then the rancher's eyes opened, shock appearing in their depths, and he tried to sit up at once, but an expression of agony came to his features and he sank back again, groaning to himself. 'What's happened to me?' he breathed.

'You were shot from behind,' Stannard answered. 'I know who did it, and we're going to make them pay.'

'Who was it?'

Stannard gave his head a quick shake. 'Everybody thinks you're dead. You and I are alone here, and only I know you're still alive. It's important that others go on believing you dead, so I'm going to try and get you upstairs to your bedroom without anybody hearing us. Can I rely on you to help me all you can?'

'Why the secrecy?' Hardiman asked.

'There's a good reason – an advantage in it for us. I'll explain it to you when we're alone.'

'I want to know all the ins-and-outs, blast it!' the cattleman mumbled obstinately. 'Whatever plans you may have, Pete Stannard, I don't see why I should creep around like a felon in my own home.'

'We'll discuss it upstairs,' Stannard said firmly, feeling mightily relieved by the fact that Hardiman's reason and will had so obviously been unimpaired by the damage to his head.

'You must trust me. I wouldn't ask it of you in this manner if it wasn't absolutely necessary. Can you accept that?'

'I trust your judgement, yes.'

'Then will you go along with it?'

'Oh, very well,' Hardiman said, a reluctance behind the thick rolling of his tongue. 'Get me upright.'

Stannard braced himself to the task, knowing that a single fall by a man of Hardiman's size would probably be heard all over the house and alert everybody there. He breathed a word of encouragement, and off the floor the rancher came, eyes staring dazedly and grunts and groans issuing from his throat at the effort of forcing his muscles and joints back into service. It was touch and go, and his helper kept a knee blocked behind the rancher's thighs to act as a seat if the effort should become too much for Hardiman, but the big man kept slowly rising and soon reached something like his full height. Now he slumped against the support of Stannard's lighter frame for the moments necessary for achieving a second wind and gathering himself for the actual crossing of the room.

They started moving ahead. Knowing there was little to gain by doing this in fits and starts, Stannard threw the whole of his body into acting as the cattleman's staff and they lurched and shuffled towards the dining room door without pause, reaching it with the rubbery knees of the rancher seeming a trifle firmer than when they had begun. Stannard made certain of the other's balance, then reopened the door and craned out into the hall and, once sure that the space was empty, helped his charge out of the dining room – careful to close up again in their wake, as some protection against the curious eyes of other occupants of the house who might possibly come this way later – and then guided the rancher over to the stairs, which were at the other side of the hall and somewhat to the left.

They halted at the foot of the broad ascent. As he gazed upwards, Stannard experienced a sinking sensation and feared that they couldn't possibly make it up to the landing above, but just then Hardiman's frame stiffened in his grasp and he realised that the cattleman was gaining strength from his efforts and undaunted by the prospect of the climb. The rancher put out a hand to the banister on his right and lifted his corresponding foot without any prompting from his helper, and up the first step they went in a clean movement – two more following in similar rhythm – and by now Stannard knew that he had only to steady his charge as and when necessary and they were going to get there in the end. And that, indeed, was how it turned out – with one laboured tread following the next all the way – and suddenly it was done and it remained only to find the resolution to cross the landing itself and enter the bedroom which Hardiman indicated as his own.

This, too, was managed without accident, and Stannard steered the rancher to his bed and helped him to stretch out upon it, plumping up the pillows behind his neck and shoulders. Then, with the big man panting from his exertions and Stannard easing his back, they gazed at each other for a minute or so before the younger man finally drew up a chair and said: 'Now.'

NINE

Stannard left the Toppling H ranch house at dawn. He and Virgil Hardiman had done a lot of talking during the night, and it was all agreed between them. Their plan was clearly worked out, and each knew what the other was going to do later in the morning. The trouble, however, was that their scheme was less than foolproof and Hardiman's physical condition was not really good enough to match the efforts required of him; but both knew that it was well nigh impossible to arrange anything in this life that was even near perfect. They could only do their best and, if their plan did fall apart, they would just have to make a fight of it and hope that they came out of it alive. Whatever happened, this was plainly their best and, perhaps, only chance of bringing Alice Mears and Cliff Sandford to justice, since success depended on the pair suddenly discovering that Hardiman was still alive. A shock line that could be achieved only once.

Sitting loosely astride his horse, Stannard headed for the south trail to Shelbyville. There was a slash of yellow light in the east now, and he was able to gaze around him in the dim and misty gleam of the rising day. He was aware that the first risk of the plan was already with him, for he was fairly sure that Sandford – who had made no move of any kind during the night – would have anticipated his early departure for town and send out at least one watcher to confirm his going. Thus, with his leaving almost certainly witnessed, it was likely that Sandford would abandon earlier restraints and try to block any move that he feared Stannard might be planning against him. Some type of misfortune on the trail could before long intervene, and it seemed only wise to stay keyed up and entirely ready for it. Though it did not have to happen thus, of course, since the ranch manager might decide that any action he regarded as necessary would be better taken in town, where Bill Stannard's nosey brother must have become a subject of talk before now and was probably already considered a dangerous nuisance to have around.

The progress of Stannard's mount become rather desultory, but he didn't stir the creature up. It was much too early in the day for all this, but he had felt it necessary to leave the ranch house before his very presence there led to questions concerning the night before and a premature search for Virgil Hardiman's body. As it was, he hoped that everybody in the house would take his absence for granted and suppose that the rancher's corpse was still lying behind the closed door of the dining room. Once the events of the day had got properly started – and Hardiman was also out of the house – the mysteries surrounding them would just have to baffle others until the doings of the day had played themselves out and provided their own explanations of what had occurred. The only thing that really mattered was that Cliff Sandford should have no inkling of the truth until too late. Stannard shivered at the thought of it all. The balance seemed too delicate; it must go down the wrong way. He had tried to be too smart. Those who dared didn't always win. Not by a long chalk!

Here again his mind seemed to have felt the shadow of the next event, for shortly after that he became aware of movement on the trail ahead. There was a rider coming towards him. Man and horse were hardening out of the dawn's gloaming like ghosts granted an extension of their tenure. The hour seemed grey and breathless; but then, as if at Stannard's prompting, the breeze wailed softly and the plains stirred, the first great land shadow of the day rippling away to the limits of sight and fading amidst broken horizons and grass without end. Stannard and the man approaching him could have been hirsute lords of an earlier time on collision course; but, as Standard pulled rein and came to a tentative halt, the man before him lifted a clenched fist and let it open theatrically, clearly calling attention to its emptiness and his own lack of any wish to harm.

The horseman was Horace Manea. Stannard fixed the other with a flinty eye. After the incident of last night – which had been a collision indeed – he had no kindly feeling towards the spidery man and would cheerfully have fought him there and then, with pistol or knuckles; but it had never been Stannard's nature to provoke violence while there was even a glimmer of goodwill from the opposition, and he folded down over his pommel watchfully and waited for Manea to stop also. Then he said: 'Let's have none of your old buck now.'

Manea leered ingratiatingly, evil personified, with his lower lip thrusting fleshily and his round eyes leaking rheum. 'Greetin's, brother.'

'T' hell!'

'I have a message from Alice Mears.'

'Oh – ah?'

'The lady is concerned for your health, suh,' Manea explained unctuously. 'She reckons you're sort o' delicate and liable to pick up the kind of illnesses we have about. She don't want you to get found dead at the trailside.'

'You get cases of lead poisoning everywhere,' Stannard replied, his voice bitter-sweet. 'I get the idea.'

'All you have to do is shape up southwards,' Manea said, smirking complacently, 'and take yourself off while you're still healthy – not forgetting that master hiding you caught off Cliff Sandford.'

'Was that how he saw it?' Stannard tut-tutted. 'I may have to change his mind about that one.'

'Don't let that give you further ideas of sticking around,' Manea warned, his tones hardening greatly. 'This is your last chance.'

'You had that last night, Horry!'

'Did I?' Manea commented. 'Dearie me!'

'You trying to say you weren't aiming to kill me?'

'If I'd meant to kill you, Stannard, you'd be dead.'

'I don't like a liar, mister, but you suit me just as well.'

'That's what I say,' Manea said resignedly. 'It'll come to it, never you fear.' A sinister grin traced itself around his eyes, yet touched no other part of his seamed and wrinkled face. 'Well, I've earned my silver dollar – and now I bid you farewell.'

'So long,' Stannard said, his adieu echoing the other's implicit mockery.

Manea bowed his mount through the tightest of equine turns, and the watching Stannard had to admit that the manoeuvre was as pretty a piece of horsemanship as any man could wish to see. Then Manea set off in the direction of Shelbyville at a tidy speed, but was no more than two hundred yards down the trail – and Stannard had barely started after him – when he cut his pace to a far more sedate trot and showed no sign of picking up the rate again. Keeping a careful eye on the spidery man, Stannard moved his horse forward at much the same gait as that ahead of him. But he was quite content that Manea should keep to his present position, for while he had the fellow in full view, a drygulching need not be expected. It was the bullet from hiding that had to be feared most, since it was the stamp of the assassin and almost impossible to guard against. This morning now seemed increasingly full of its threat. Indeed, that was what the recent warning had been about. Stannard realised that his enemies were up to something, but he wasn't sure exactly what.

The procession of two continued, and mists fluffed about the rawness of the trail and increased Stannard's sense of isolation, bringing a chill to his flesh and tension to his gut. The length of the ride into town, short enough in all conscience, seemed to exaggerate – even to go on beyond anything natural – and Stannard was beginning to wonder whether he could be trapped in a ride outside time, when the trail curved left and the walls and rooftops of Shelbyville became visible as a sprawling presence under the northern sky.

Stannard stretched himself against his stirrups, his entire saddle cracking and creaking under his buttocks, old leather and dry strings, and his breath came and went in sighing, irregular blurts. He was like a man emerging from a doze that had seemed full waking, and everything jolted into true focus as he perceived that Manea had just used his spurs and was now receding swiftly down Shelbyville's main street. He appeared to be making for the Gunpowder saloon, and Stannard let it go at that; for his first business was with the sheriff and, if Joe Temple wasn't in his office, he would have to root the lawman out at his home address, which Virgil Hardiman had earlier supplied.

Still making no better than a trot, Stannard approached the first building at this end of town, a derelict warehouse situated on his left; and, as he gazed at the structure's glassless windows, nailed-up doorways and crumbling, mildewed walls, he was abruptly conscious of a threat. There was nothing visible, but his horse confirmed his intimation of danger by puckering its hide and staggering across its line of tread, as if fearing to go on. Stannard, already more intimidated than he would have cared to admit – and now seeing the pernicious Manea as no better than a bell-wether – was in no mood to play the hero but bent over his mount's neck and sprang straight to the ground, landing whole-footed and jerking his revolver in the instant that a rifle flashed down at him from a window-space high up in the old building adjacent and a bullet whizzed several inches above his crown, a certain hit in his upper body if he had stayed in the saddle.

Stannard knelt into the smallest target that he could make. He rather expected that the one shot would be followed by the bushwhacker's flight; but, contrary to this, the morning hush was split wide open by a string of cracking detonations as a series of slugs – angrily pumped out by the forced mechanism of a repeating rifle – beat the earth all around the crouched Stannard and left him leading the proverbial charmed life in their midst.

The fusillade ceased as abruptly as it had begun, a tiny click from above telling of an empty magazine, and Stannard came up with mouth hard and pistol levelled, the side of his left hand chopping off another ripping blast of explosions in the direction of the space from which he had seen the rifle flashing down into the street. Woodwork flew apart up there, dissolving into dark fragments that floated a little as they came drifting downwards, and Stannard glimpsed rapid movements behind the churning impact of the slugs but judged that he had scored no hit and that his would-be killer was now retreating into the rear of the room which he occupied and about to join a pre-planned escape route that would bring him down through the building and out onto the lots at the back of the place.

Stannard was again enraged. It seemed that of late nothing but cowardly attacks had been made on him, and this was another one. He wanted revenge or satisfaction, and he rushed at the nearest of the roughly sealed doors along the street level of the building's front and took a flying kick at it, expecting the force of the impact to tear out the crosswork of planking that held the door shut, but the seal resisted his effort and threw him backwards and onto his seat. He picked himself up, swearing, but had no more than essayed his second attempt to break into the warehouse, when a peremptory shout from a short distance up the street made him think again, and he stood back and gazed to his right, seeing the huge figure of Sheriff Joe Temple heading for him at a lumbering run. 'What the hell do you think you're up to?' the lawman demanded, his wrath adding great force to the prosaic wording of his question. 'You're a bane to this town!'

'Haven't you got eyes in your head?' Stannard yelled back. 'Somebody just tried to kill me! You try being reasonable, mister!'

Temple came to a halt about two paces short of where Stannard was standing. 'Don't you tell me – !'

'Should we leg it round the back?' Stannard interrupted. 'It's normal to chase bushwhackers!'

'Shut up!' Temple snorted in reply. 'Oh, come on then! Let's find out what you're made of!'

They sprang round and began running. At the end of the warehouse up street of them, an alley was visible. They entered this narrow way, and down its length they hammered, emerging on the lots at its end. Jerking to a halt, they peered this way and that – both already blowing a little – but there was nobody in sight and not a whisper of fleeing footfalls to be heard.

On their left, in the back of the abandoned building, was an open door from which bits of wet rubbish had been kicked away by flying feet. Stannard and the lawman went to the entrance and peered inside. Beyond it was a stairway. This they climbed with a curious mixture of blurting rashness and abrupt caution, entering at the top a bare, damp-stained room which stank of gunsmoke. Sure now that the bushwhacker was long gone from this vantage, they went to the window opposite – where the stench of firing was thickest – and gazed down and out at the spot below on which Stannard had so nearly met his death a minute or two ago. Then, withdrawing their heads, they gazed down at the floor under the sill, where the lawman had just set a crunching boot amidst the several cartridge cases lying there. Letting out a growling sigh, he said: 'I wonder?'

'I'll bet you do,' Stannard agreed ironically, for he was as little mollified just now as the other appeared.

Joe Temple spat out what seemed to be a nasty taste. 'I can put up with that brother of yours ahead of you any day!'

'Goes to prove you've got some sense,' Stannard responded.

'Enough of that,' the lawman cautioned.

Stannard smiled wryly. 'What were you wondering?'

'If I still had a single valid doubt that there's been something going on in this district that I'd never dreamed of before yesterday evening,' Joe Temple confessed. 'I was also wondering who it was first shot at you.'

'Well, it wasn't Horry Manea,' Stannard said. 'That hellion rode into town right straight ahead of me – and he passed this muckhole by. How about Alice Mears? I happen to know she's handy with a rifle. Or does she have other retainers of the Manea ilk around her place?'

'Alice does have other bad lots around the Gunpowder saloon,' Temple replied. 'But it may interest you to know that Cliff Sandford and those two monkeys of his, Hengel and Smith, are in town. A patrolling deputy of mine saw them go into Alice's drinking house during the early hours.'

'Ah, now,' Stannard murmured thoughtfully. 'Yes, that is interesting. Has Cliff Sandford been in to see you yet?'

'What about?' the sheriff queried.

'So he hasn't,' Stannard reflected. 'I reckon they were hoping to get me first – one way or the other.'

'Don't hold anything back from me,' the lawman counselled. 'What are you here for this morning, Stannard? I can think of reasons why you should have come into Shelbyville, but I want to hear your own.'

'I hope to make Alice Mears confess that she murdered my sister-in-law.'

'Make?' Temple echoed. 'You've some hopes of

that!'

'I'll get her to talk somehow.'

'Whether she's guilty of anything or not,' the sheriff said, 'you'll need a mighty smart argument to do much good with her.'

'It has to be tried,' Stannard responded. 'You know that old saying, Sheriff: "The guilty need no accusing". I figure even that Mears woman is subject to it – once confronted with the whole of her crimes; and that includes the things she thinks we can't know.'

'Even so,' Temple sighed, still clearly doubting. 'If any of this is to help your brother – and I know that's all you're really interested in – cleverer men than I will need to be convinced.'

'Alice may be the hard nut you suggest,' Stannard said, 'but she has accomplices who don't measure up to her. And I'm not sure the principal one was a completely willing dupe to start with, while —'

'Sandford?' Temple interjected.

Stannard nodded. 'The rest are dull as dishwater – if wicked enough to play hell.'

'I want to see this,' the sheriff admitted. 'I'm not sure I believe in it, and I can see real trouble ahead – maybe shooting trouble – so I'm giving you the chance here and now to think again before you go blundering into something that could put you in the dock. The more serious the accusation, Stannard, the better the proof has to be.'

'I understand that,' Stannard assured him, 'and I don't need to think again.'

'Let's go then,' Temple said shortly. 'The Gunpowder saloon is the only place this can be sorted out.'

'Mighty glad of your company,' Stannard returned. 'I was preparing to seek it just before you came on me.'

The sheriff said in jaundiced tones that he was glad to hear it, and they withdrew from the derelict warehouse. Regaining the street out front, they headed for the Gunpowder saloon – Stannard walking his horse – and en route they passed windows at which the drapes twitched as they were eyed stealthily by citizens who were obviously curious about gunfire at this hour and no doubt judging instinctively from the sheriff's presence and the general atmosphere that serious doings were afoot. Joe Temple scowled a time or two at the watchers, then looked straight ahead, but Stannard allowed his interest to go unchecked, for the wariness of his earlier mood had not abated one bit. A single mistake and a man was dead. The rule was unfailing, and applied as much at this moment as it had at any other. From death no man ever returned; there were no second chances when the killer gun shot straight.

They arrived outside Alice Mears' saloon. Stannard quickly secured his mount at the hitching rail, then he and the sheriff marched on the batwings and shouldered indoors. Stannard immediately noted that only Alice Mears herself and the men concerned in his business were present. They sat pale and sweaty in the pallid light of the room, for the new day was now bright at the windows and the light of the lamps hanging from the ceiling above had little influence against the power of the rising sun. The blonde saloon woman, well-painted and a-toss with fine braids, was lounging on her left elbow at the bar and showing a lovely turn of calf below the knee-length hem of her pleated yellow silk dress, while Clifford Sandford, Bart Hengel and John Smith, were again seated at the big table which occupied the room's centre. Horry Manea, droopy-lidded and twitchy, was also at the spot where Stannard had seen him before – outside the door which led to Alice's living rooms at the back of the building – and his spidery presence was made the more sinister by the manner in which he kept letting his fingertips creep up and down the top of his thighs and laughing to himself at secret thoughts.

'Good morning, gentlemen,' Alice Mears said, her eyes challenging as she drew herself erect and folded her arms under her breasts. 'I won't ask what I can get you from behind the bar.'

'Don't, Alice,' the sheriff agreed. 'I'm on duty here, and Pete Stannard is part of it.'

'What do you want?' the woman inquired.

'You murdered my sister-in-law,' Stannard accused.

'Merle was my best friend,' Alice Mears said

dismissively. 'It isn't any good, Mr Stannard. That brother of yours is going to hang tomorrow. You can't get him off. I think you've come here with the intention of bearing false witness, and that is shameful.'

'Merle was also Cliff Sandford's woman,' Stannard said, ignoring the rest of the words spoken by Alice Mears. 'She supplanted you in his affections.'

'Fancy words,' the blonde scoffed. 'Merle and I shared other men also. What's so unusual about that?'

'Only that you were as angry about Merle taking your place in Sandford's affections as he was about Luke Barnes taking his place in hers.'

'Rubbish!'

'Sandford hired Eli Bazzarin to assassinate Warnes, didn't he?' Stannard went on. 'But you were afraid Sandford would foul up and get himself hanged if he tried that one; so you killed Merle yourself to shield him from the risk and put Eli Bazzarin on a retaining fee – because you were already pondering a target for him yourself.'

'When you use my name,' Sandford said icily, 'you should address the business involved with it to me.'

'I'm coming to you,' Stannard said. 'It was Virgil Hardiman who really broke you and Merle up, wasn't it? He was ashamed of how his illegitimate daughter was dishonouring her marriage vows and destroying my brother, his friend. So Hardiman threatened to take you out of his Will, and leave the Toppling H, which was to have been yours, to Merle instead, giving her both his money and his property.'

'More rubbish!' Sandford jeered. 'There's no means by which you can know any of this!'

'Merle, not realising Alice Mears' underlying enmity, told her friend all about this,' Stannard went on remorselessly, 'and Alice reckoned she could put your affairs straight again by having Virgil Hardiman bushwhacked – since the rancher had been the target for Bazzarin that I mentioned just now. Only I happened to intervene at this point and, not to make too much of it, I think Alice saw me climb down the well on the waste ground behind this saloon – in search of a brass candlestick which I found – and realised that I was already getting near the truth. That being so, she sent Bazzarin to gun me down, only he failed to make a job of it and, knowing that I had some inkling of his identity and would soon catch up with him and extract a lot of the truth from him, she saw that she would have to kill him for herself in order to shut his mouth. And that was what she did.

'Later, discovering that I had made the acquaintance of Virgil Hardiman – and fearing what he could tell me about the matters in the background of his daughter's life that concerned him – she decided that the rancher would have to die at once, and by her hand. So she rode out to the Toppling H last night – having already despatched Horry Manea to warn Cliff

Sandford of what was coming – and bushwhacked Hardiman while he and I were eating dinner together in his dining room. That makes Alice Mears guilty of triple murder, and Sandford guilty of complicity in all her crimes.'

'I was nowhere near the Toppling H last night,' Alice Mears said. 'I went for a ride close by to get a little exercise, that's all.'

'First things first,' Sheriff Temple cut in at once. 'Is Virgil Hardiman dead?'

'That's what I came into town to report,' Sandford said glibly. 'Yes, he's dead. I was just giving you the chance to get out of your bed and back to work, Sheriff. That's why I delayed visiting your office.'

'Okay,' Temple said slowly. 'You seem able to account for yourself in that respect. But there's a pattern here, an' it fits a lot of worrying facts. What do you say to that, Alice? How much did Merle Stannard tell you about her private affairs?'

'She told me nothing,' Alice Mears said boldly. 'You prove those private things, Sheriff. Stannard regards them as the motive for most of the crimes he says I've committed? Merle's dead, and her father is dead. Who is there to answer now for what he did or didn't do, Joe Temple?'

'I can answer!' a male voice boomed, and Virgil Hardiman himself thrust open the batwings and stepped into the saloon. 'I can endorse every word Pete Stannard has spoken!'

Alice Mears looked utterly stunned. It seemed to Stannard that the silence became absolute, and that everybody present had turned to stone.

TEN

Staying alert to the whole scene, but far from sure of what was coming next, Stannard tucked his thumbs into the front of his gunbelt and simply stood there waiting.

It was Alice Mears who shook off the general paralysis first and said: 'Risen from the grave, Virgil?'

'You tried hard enough to put me there, Alice,' Hardiman replied grimly, touching the raw wound on the right side of his head. 'You're a dirty backshooter!'

'Prove it,' she taunted.

'I ran after you out there on the grass, Alice,' Stannard reminded. 'I came near pulling you down, too, but your luck held.'

'It wasn't a question of luck,' the blonde said brazenly. 'I wasn't there, you mistook me for somebody else. All this is being unloaded on me, Sheriff. Pete Stannard will do or say anything to save that brother of his from the hangman. You can see that for yourself. You may be a lot of things but you're not a fool.'

'I've said it once,' the lawman returned. 'The story we've just heard from Stannard fits a lot of the known facts.'

Alice Mears twitched a shoulder disdainfully. 'Pete Stannard is a smart son-of-a-bitch, I'll give him that, and he's shaped what looks like guilt out of events that we all know happened otherwise. We lived through the days and things that were done. It's our story, Sheriff. You were happy enough with it before Stannard began bending it about.'

'Maybe,' Joe Temple conceded. 'But the wound I see on Mr Hardiman is real enough, and somebody tried to shoot Pete Stannard a few minutes ago – almost under my eyes.'

'But not quite, eh?' Alice Mears countered narrowly. 'Anybody could have tried to kill him. He's made few friends around here.' She laughed spitefully. 'Yes, Joe Temple, I can see it in your face. You're beginning to realise that you can't actually prove a single damned thing. That's what I've been telling you all along.'

'Trying to persuade me of more likely,' the lawman corrected.

'Matter of interpretation, maybe?' the woman suggested.

'Alice, you're being crafty with words.'

'The truth is the truth, Joe, whatever the words

used to tell it.'

Stannard knew that some comment was expected from him, but he had been no more than half listening to the speakers during the last few moments. His eyes had gone down and fixed on the boots of the three men sitting at the room's middle table. Those on the feet of Bart Hengel and John Smith were clean enough, but Cliff Sandford's were scratched and dirty at the toes, also visibly damp. This brought back to Stannard's mind the little swathes of rubbish which had been kicked away from the door which the sheriff and he had entered at the back of the derelict warehouse. It required no great stretch of the imagination to conclude that it had been Sandford's boots which had kicked aside the refuse from the rotting threshold back there, since there was similar dirt clinging around the welts of his own footwear – and Joe Temple's likewise. 'It was you who fired on me as I rode into Shelbyville a short while ago, Sandford,' he accused crisply. 'Look at your boots, man! Sheriff, look at yours and mine. See what I mean? Remember that muck outside the back door of the old warehouse?'

Sandford rose like a jack-in-the-box. 'That's it!' he declared. 'I'm putting up with no more of this. Bart – John; up you get! We'll be into charades next. Alice is exactly right. Nothing's happened but what Stannard talked it up! In a world that was properly run, Tod Hempnall would hang both the Stannard brothers tomorrow at noon.' Now he jerked his head at the risen Hengel and Smith. 'Let's go! Mr Hardiman is still alive, praise be to the Lord, so we've no longer any purpose here.'

'Hold it right where you are, Sandford!' the sheriff warned. 'You're not going anywhere yet awhile.'

'I'm in his way too,' Virgil Hardiman reminded flatly. 'Whatever happens, Clifford, you're finished at the Toppling H. I've put up with many times what I ought to have stood from you across the years. It's all gone – ranch and money alike. You can look to nothing more from me.'

'Then god-damn your soul, you fat and ugly old toad!' Sandford snarled. 'We're still leaving, boys. They can't stop us. They've nothing to go on. They'll be breaking the law themselves if they try to hold us, and they can't hold Alice either. Not on that bullshit about Hardiman's Will and what Merle Stannard did or didn't tell her. No, sirree! So let Joe Temple forage how he likes, and Virgil Hardiman talk as big as he always does!'

Suddenly there was a revolver in the sheriff's hand. 'Nobody leaves!' he announced sternly.

'That ain't right,' John Smith complained. 'What have the foreman and I done wrong?'

'Guilt by association,' Bart Hengel explained, his tough features all screwed up.

'You keep your mouths shut!' Sandford ordered.

'Say what you like,' Hardiman put in, 'but don't

move an inch. I pay your wages, men.'

'I'm going to lock you all up!' the sheriff fumed. 'And that's how you're liable to stay until we've had a properly conducted inquiry into the new evidence we have in the Bill Stannard case.'

'Can't you get anything through your thick skull, Joe?' Alice Mears demanded in her pert and cocksure manner. 'You don't have any new evidence. At best it's speculative – at worst it's fictional. You've got to have something more to go on than a loud mouthed Virg Hardiman and a pair of dirty boots!'

'Keep out of it, Alice!' Sandford warned.

'We can beat them, Cliff!' the saloon woman begged. 'You must hold firm!'

'For you?' Sandford virtually hissed at her. 'It's all gone for me. You dragged me into your scheming, blast your jealous, greedy eyes, and now I've lost everything! I forgave you Merle, but I'm not going to rot in jail for you. I'm out of here!' He seized the edge of the tabletop before him and heaved at the heavy piece of furniture with all his strength, tipping it into a spin that sent it tumbling into the quarter of the room nearest the batwings. Stannard, the sheriff, and Virgil Hardiman were forced to leap aside as the table rolled among them, and Sandford took his chance to reach inside his coat and draw the revolver which he had been keeping hidden there.

'Cliff, you fool!' Alice Mears screeched, leaping forward and kicking the weapon out of his grasp.

Then she turned her head towards the doorway beside which the spidery Manea was sitting. 'Stop him, Horry!'

Manea's lank frame drew together. He rose from his chair with a Colt now filling his right fist. He aimed at Sandford – appearing about to shoot him, though perhaps only to cover him – but it seemed that somebody was not going to take a chance on it, for a gun exploded over to the spidery one's left, where Smith and Hengel had fetched up after the table had been toppled away from them, and he lurched backwards as a slug punched through his forehead and laid him low – though triggering wide of his original target at the same time – and Alice Mears cried out and clutched at her chest, sinking to her knees with blood spilling through her fingers. For a few moments she gazed at the floor, clearly fighting the pain of her wound, and then she looked up, her face grey and ghastly and said: 'I'm done for, boys!'

'You two, put a couple of tables together,' the sheriff ordered, snapping his fingers at John Smith and Bart Hengel, the former of whom was just holstering his still smoking pistol and looking a bit sheepish about what he had done. 'Out of the way now. I'm going to lift her up and place her on top.'

'Cliff,' the dying woman gasped, as Joe Temple raised her from the floor. 'I want Cliff!'

Stannard quickly glanced up and around. He saw that Sandford was on the move. The deposed ranch manager was skirting wide and obviously trying to reach the batwings and the horses at the hitching rail beyond. Now Stannard sprang into action also. He bounded across the room – absorbing two desperate punches which the fugitive threw at him as he cut the other's escape route – and then he walked into Sandford and whaled him unmercifully, pounding his ribs, bruising his belly, and thumping at his jaw with hooks and crosses which the recipient was already too weakened to block or duck beneath in any way. Then, with Sandford sagging at the knees and only just short of unconsciousness, he grabbed the man from behind and wrapped his arms around his defeated enemy's midriff, more or less carrying the deposed ranch manager after that over to the improvised resting place where Alice Mears was now lying. 'There he is, woman!' Stannard panted, seeing that the blonde's eyes were now fading and that there was a scarlet froth about her lips. 'Was it worth it? It's cost you – your life!'

'Be a little kind, Pete,' the watching Hardiman urged. 'It takes a loving woman to end up in a tragedy like this. What, for heaven's sake, is love?'

'Dunno,' Stannard said, shaking his head briefly; for he had never been able to figure that one out for himself. There was too much of the body in it to be more than an animal need. Yet it had to be more than that. A man had died on a cross in its name and poets and the like had been caterwauling down the centuries about it! The dullest of humanity would tell you it made the world go round and brighten up at the very thought. 'Confess, Alice. You killed Merle, didn't you?'

The failing saloon woman smiled a smile that was faint and cruel. Something in her stare taunted, and it looked as if she had no intention of making any admission at all.

'You've finished with this world, Alice,' Hardiman said in a quiet voice. 'Give yourself a chance in the next. If you die with your evil unrepented, you'll dance in hellfire, ugly and screaming. The damned live in black hatred and beyond all hope. You're still worth more than that, Alice – and where would it leave you with Cliff? You'd never see him again forever.'

The argument seemed a weak one to Stannard. He rather felt that the correct punishment for the apparently impenitent Alice Mears would be to suffer the shackling of an eternal union with Clifford Sandford. Even so the words did seem to carry great weight with the mortally wounded blonde, for she twitched a finger towards the watching Joe Temple and said in a barely audible whisper: 'I – I brained Merle with that candlestick, Joe. The little ninny took Cliff away from me, and – and I wanted my – revenge.' Then a blank stare entered the woman's eyes and her lips fell silent.

'She's gone,' Hardiman said.

The sheriff nodded gravely. 'You all heard what she told me. I reckon her words count as a deathbed confession. There'll have to be sworn statements, of course, but it's my belief—'

'My brother is now in the clear?' Stannard queried.

'I think it's safe to say that,' the lawman replied. 'I don't like you a lot, mister, and I know you don't care much for me; but you're a sticker, I've got to say that for you. You stick like glue. Twelve hours ago, I wouldn't have given a cat's chance in hell of proving your brother innocent. It looked an open and shut case against him. But you've sure as heck shown the flaws in that. There's got to be a lesson there somewhere. What can you ever be entirely sure about?'

'It was just a matter of keeping the faith,' Stannard said, knowing that he had not been a hundred percent at it. 'Men don't change much, and I had absolute trust in my brother. I was bound to do all I could for him.'

'That's what you did,' the lawman assured him. 'I hope he appreciates it.'

'I don't much care if he doesn't,' Stannard answered. 'He'll live, Sheriff, and that's all that matters.'

'Sure.'

'Can I see Bill now?'

'You'd like to break the good news, eh?'

'I reckon that's about the size of it,' Stannard

admitted.

'Nobody has a better right,' Joe Temple said. 'You can talk to Bill as long as you want when we've got Sandford locked up where he belongs.'

'March!' Stannard ordered, pointing Sandford towards the batwings and giving him a shove between the shoulder-blades.

Eyes down, the prisoner moved ahead without a murmur. He didn't even glance back at the corpse of the woman who had been prepared to risk so much for him while gaining her own revenge. There could be no joy in evil; only suffering. On the other hand, you could make a ride to the gallows with an innocent heart and find happiness at the end. He and Bill were going to have that evening he had promised himself, and if they got pie-eyed – so what?